SCENT of DECEIT

A Novel

D1495541

AALIYAH SHALAWN

STREET *Essence*

Published by:

G Street Chronicles
P.O. Box 1822
Jonesboro, GA 30237-1822
www.gstreetchronicles.com
fans@gstreetchronicles.com

Cover design:
Hot Book Covers, www.hotbookcovers.com

ISBN 13: 978-1-9384424-8-3
ISBN 10: 1938442482
LCCN: 2013931241

Join us on our social networks

Facebook
G Street Chronicles Fan Page
G Street Chronicles CEO Exclusive Readers Group

Follow us on Twitter
@GStreetChronicl

Acknowledgements

I would like to thank everyone who supported this journey…I thank GOD everyday for the special people in my life, who love me unconditionally.

I am thankful for my living angel, my mother Linda, who not only taught me how to be a woman and a mother, but has been there for me and helped me through every up and down of my life. I am blessed to have such a musically gifted and creative father, Michael, who ignited my inner writer as a young child. I love my parents dearly. To my big brother Mike, his consistency and hard work has always been what I admired the most about him. His successes have always motivated me to work hard, and I love him for it.

I can't explain the love that I have for Khaalidah, Kymaani, Tylan, Taj and Saudiah, my children. They are my inspiration; their energy is everything and more. They each motivate me in different ways. They are talented, beautiful and my reasons for accomplishing my dreams. Mommy loves you all.

To my husband Antonio bka Babe…knowing that I could always be myself with you, express my feelings exactly as they were, tell you every idea I've ever had, (and we know that's every other week…lol) and you still supported me, and elaborated on it all means a lot. You have always presented and promoted me in every endeavor and that means so much. You are an amazing talented man, and together our family will win. I love you.

Victoria Valentin, you have been a mentor and a friend. I will always remember when you told me that I had wonderful ideas and that I was very creative, "But you never follow through with action." As much as it hurt to hear, it hurt as much as it helped. I am forever grateful for your ability to keep it "real" with me chica.

Shiron Bell girlfriend, how do I thank you for just being an honest and true friend. Before I am a writer, I am a woman and a mother and you've always cared about the bond that we built based on being mothers and women. You are genuine and I love you for that.

CHAPTER 1

It was an unusually warm November afternoon, and salon owner Selena Nichols was in the middle of a sew-in weave on one of her regular clients. Kouture Kuts was the crème de la crème of high-end salons in Philadelphia. Selena was the owner and the only stylist in the salon. She had a receptionist and a makeup artist who worked out of the salon, but no other stylists. That was the way it had been since the doors opened six years ago, and that's the way it would remain. Selena never associated herself with many females besides her sister and a couple of long-time clients who she would occasionally join for cocktails.

The salon was decorated in various shades of pink, accented with scented candles, fresh flowers and beautiful chandeliers. The stylist station was on a raised section of the salon, while the clients who waited sat in what looked like a talk show audience. Plasma televisions and portraits of famous pin-up dolls adorned the walls. Selena was into the Hollywood Glamour era. When she bought the building, her sister Tamara, an interior decorator, made her dreams come true.

On this particular Saturday, Selena had arrived at about 7 a.m. and performed her usual morning ritual of starting her top-of-the-line coffee machine and arranging fresh donuts, fruit, and bottled water for her clients. Selena was originally a business major at Temple University, and used various marketing strategies in her salon to obtain and maintain clients.

Once the continental breakfast was on display, Selena would most likely be found in the mirror putting finishing touches on her bronze chin length bob, or touching up her M•A•C lip-gloss. Selena was big on appearance, and never believed the old 'stylists never have time to do their own hair' speech. She sprayed a little more of her favorite fragrance, Emilio Pucci, and the salon doors were unlocked.

It was around 11 a.m., and Selena was about 20 minutes away from finishing Andrea's weave. There were four other clients in the salon at the time. The makeup artist, Danielle, was performing a pre-wedding consultation on a client, while two other women watched The View and sipped coffee in the waiting area. Arielle, Selena's fifteen-year-old niece, was at the front desk texting away on her Blackberry. She came in on Friday evenings and Saturday mornings, to help her aunt out with the phones and scheduling appointments.

As soon as Selena had finished the last curl in Andrea's hair, a woman walked in the front door. It immediately alarmed Selena because the clients who were in the salon were the only clients booked for the day. She had purposely scheduled a half-day. Her fiancé, Sean, was taking her to a comedy show in Atlantic City, and she was looking forward to it.

She and Sean hadn't been out in a while. Sean was a police officer. Lately, he had to take on more hours to cover for the shortage of officers. The city had to do some lay-offs because of budget restraints. It had been about three weeks since they'd been out, but it felt like months to Selena. She and Sean were a young couple who both had decent careers and no children. They loved to go out and take vacations.

Selena mumbled under her breath to Andrea, "I hope she knows I don't take walk-ins."

Andrea chuckled as they watched the woman talk to Arielle at the front desk. Arielle gestured in Selena's direction, and the woman walked towards her. Selena began to feel a little bad. The woman appeared to be very pregnant, and she would hate to turn away someone who was expecting. But that getaway to Atlantic City with her future husband was calling her name.

The woman walked over and introduced herself as Nadiyah. Selena greeted the woman and asked how she could help her as she studied her and guessed that Nadiyah couldn't be older than twenty-one.

She looked Selena in her eyes. "I couldn't continue to be silent about this any longer. My child will never come second to you or anyone else."

Selena put her flat irons down, excused herself from her client, and asked Nadiyah to step into her office. She had no idea who this woman was, or what she was talking about.

"I'm sorry. Do I know you?" Selena asked once they were in the office.

Nadiyah explained. "No you don't, but I know you. Like I said, my child will never come second, and since her father could not be a man and let you know about us, here I am."

Selena felt weak. She started to feel hot all over, and immediately looked out in the salon to see if anyone had heard anything. All of the clients sat patiently waiting, so Selena began to question the woman.

"What are you talking about? Who is her father? And what do I have to do with this?"

In her heart, Selena already knew the answers to the questions, but she needed to hear the words come out of this woman's mouth.

Within seconds, she got her wish. She explained to Selena that she was 7 months pregnant with Sean's child, and that they had been seeing each other for the last two of the six years that she and Sean had been together. Nadiyah explained that for the first year, she knew nothing about her; Sean had lied. She only found out a year ago, because a client of Selena's who happened to be Nadiyah's friend, saw a picture of Sean and Selena hanging on Selena's station at the salon.

"Once my friend told me, I questioned Sean about you. He initially denied your relationship as nothing serious, but I knew it had to be more. I started to notice his patterns and dug a little deeper. I followed him here one evening. He was happy to see you when you came out of the shop. Y'all kissed, and you hopped on the back of his bike. I sat and watched the two of you ride off. By then, I was already in love, and as much as I tried, I just could not leave him alone. Now here I am pregnant and alone. He told me three weeks ago, that he would always send financial support for the baby, but he didn't want anything to do with me or her because he was marrying you."

Both women stood in silence, tears dropping from their eyes. Selena simply thanked Nadiyah for the information and asked her to leave.

Nadiyah obliged and whispered a simple, "I'm sorry"

as she walked out of Selena's office.

Selena wiped her tears, walked back to her station, and continued on as if nothing happened. Selena was never the type to talk to her clients about her personal business, so it didn't seem odd that she never said a word about what the woman said to her. Inside, however, she felt every possible emotion she could feel; hurt, anger, sadness and betrayal, to name a few.

Selena left work at four o'clock that afternoon and dropped her niece off at a friend's house not too far from the salon. She immediately called her sister, Tamara, to tell her about what happened. Tamara was at a loss for words. Selena wept for almost an hour on the phone. She was more than just her sister; she was her best friend. Tamara was the only other person, besides Sean, that she confided in and showed her emotions to.

The sisters were not rowdy or troublemakers, but this information made Selena extremely upset. She wanted to take action against Sean and his pregnant mistress. Tamara quickly brought her back to reality. She explained that it wouldn't prove anything to resort to violence and that she had too much to lose, including her dignity and reputation. Selena agreed, but the tears would not stop falling.

"I will meet you at your house in fifteen minutes, Lena."

"No, I need to handle this alone. I'm fine. I'll call you later."

The phone went dead as Tamara sat in her kitchen, contemplating whether to respect her sister's wishes, or to disregard them and be by her side through this.

It was almost 6 p.m. when Selena pulled into the driveway of the townhome that she shared with Sean in the

Greater Northeast section of the city. She had ignored seven calls from Sean during the ride home, and felt nauseous at the thought of seeing his face. She turned the key and walked in silently.

Sean yelled out from upstairs over the loud music coming from the speakers in the sitting room. "Leen, what's up babe, is your phone dead? I was worried about you. I'll start the shower for you. The show starts in an hour and a half, and you know how long you take to get ready."

Selena remained silent and walked into her beautiful kitchen full of stainless steel appliances, and marble countertops. She began to cry again as she opened a bottle of Moscato and poured herself a glass. As she tipped the glass up to her lips to take a sip, Sean yelled again.

"Selena, what are you doing? You hear me talking to you?"

Selena threw the glass against the wall and began to run up the staircase, screaming and crying uncontrollably.

"How could you do this to me!" she yelled.

Sean grabbed her and tried to calm her down. He had no idea what was going on.

"So she didn't let you know she came to my place of employment with a round belly, a belly that she says you helped with? What the fuck, Sean? We are getting married. Wait a minute we WERE getting married—"

Sean interrupted. "Baby wait, let me explain."

"Explain what, Sean? After 6 years, buying a home together, and planning a wedding, you give it all up for someone else?"

"I didn't give it up. I am not going anywhere. I don't even know if the baby is mine."

"Oh, so that is supposed to fuckin' make me feel better

because you don't *think* the baby is yours? It shouldn't even be a question. You betrayed me, and I really don't care if it's your baby or not. You slept with her unprotected, jeopardizing *my life*! Get the fuck out Sean!"

Sean grabbed Selena and pushed her against the wall while she screamed for him to get off her. He knew the type of woman Selena was—this could very well be his last opportunity to explain anything, or get her to even think of working through his messy mistake. He looked deep in Selena's eyes and began to speak.

"Listen to me. I know I fucked up. I'm human. But you cannot stand here and look at me…"

Selena looked away. She couldn't deny her love for Sean. He was everything she had ever wished for in a man.

He grabbed her face and pressed his forehead to hers. "You can't act like you don't know we are perfect together. We finish each other's sentences. We're both ambitious, and we know exactly what to do to brighten each other's day, and Leen, making love to you is—"

Selena snatched away and slapped Sean in his face.

"Don't even come at me with that bullshit, because if any of that meant anything to you, you wouldn't have a fuckin' baby on the way. How could you? We planned when we would have both of *our* children together. We picked out names. Do you remember that Sean? Huh, do you? What about Miyani and Malachi? What were you thinking? Do you know how embarrassing this shit is?"

Selena walked away, but Sean grabbed her arm and began to yell. "Who the fuck cares about what people think, Leen? This is about us. We have to live with this. Stop worrying about what people would say."

"How the fuck do you sound? I don't have to live

with this. As a matter of fact, I'm not living with this. You decided to step out on me. I'm not even going to pretend that I wouldn't look at that baby differently if we stayed together. I can't do this! This bitch came to my business, in front of my clients, with this shit. I'm done!"

She walked past Sean, and before he could reach out to grab her, she screamed at him. "Do not fucking touch me!"

She grabbed her keys and looked back at Sean one more time before she yanked her two-carat engagement ring off, threw it at him, and walked out the door. She hopped into her black X5 while Sean stood in the doorway and watched as she backed out of the driveway and sped off into the darkness.

Selena had no specific destination in mind, but she knew that with Tamara, she would at least have a shoulder to cry on. She arrived at her sister's Gladwyne home in about twenty minutes. She used her key to let herself in. Tamara was a single mother, and Selena was the only family she had left after their Nana passed away four years ago.

When she heard the door close, Tamara knew it was her sister. She yelled down to her from her bedroom. "Leeni, I'm up here!"

Selena kicked her tan Valentino boots off at the door and made her way up to the bedroom. Tamara waited at the door and greeted her sister with a huge hug. Selena walked over to her sister's king sized bed, which was decorated in shades of purple, and fell back.

"Now I love you to death, but you know I don't play that shit. Get off my bed in your street clothes."

She looked over at Selena, crossed her arms, and tilted her head with a slight attitude. Selena sat up. She couldn't control her emotions. She was laughing at her sister, but crying about Sean at the same time.

"Leeni, come here. It's going to be okay."

She held her sister tightly in her arms.

Selena pulled back and immediately wiped her eyes. "Where is Arielle? I don't need her seeing me cry. She doesn't need to know about this."

"Of course not. It's Saturday night, and you know how those teenagers are. She's still where you dropped her off earlier. She's staying over Kierra's house, so come on, let those tears flow."

They both let out a little chuckle as Tamara got up to walk downstairs.

"Come on, Leeni. Let's pour us a glass of something and figure out what the next move is. I know you ain't getting back with him after this stunt."

Even though Selena did not intend to try to make it work, it still saddened her to hear the actual words. They walked into the kitchen, and Tamara opened up a bottle of Nuvo and filled their flutes to the rim. There was an awkward silence in the room, which was unusual for the two sisters who had helped each other through so much in their lives.

Tamara broke the silence as she took her third sip of the sweet pink champagne.

"So what did Sean have to say?"

"A whole lot of nothing. He tried to act as if we could work through this, and he kept saying that he loves me. But T, all I could see was a baby that wasn't ours who would have to be a part of our lives forever, including holidays, birthdays, all of that. It's not like it was a child who was there before me. He had this baby on me. I just walked out on him."

Tamara nodded her head in agreement. "Listen, you are my heart, and although we are fully grown women, you will always be my little sister. I'm always going to support you and be by your side, so whatever you decide to do is your decision. I honestly think that in order for you to make that decision clearly, you need to get away. Well, *we* need to get away."

"Get away?"

"Yes girl! You and I, on a trip. We haven't been away together since forever. It will be perfect. You know Ari leaves next week to stay with her dad for the Thanksgiving break. We could easily take a mini vacay to somewhere sunny and hot."

It sounded like just what Selena needed, but she had a million and one thoughts in her head. She could barely focus as she tried to think of an excuse not to go.

"What about the salon?"

"What about it? We don't have to leave until next week. The same way I'm gonna call my clients and let them know I'm not going to be here, is the same exact thing you're gonna do. No ifs, ands, or buts."

Selena hesitated for a moment and then gave her sister a big grin before she hi-fived her. "Alright, I'm in. Where are we going?"

"Jamaica, mon," answered Tamara.

CHAPTER 2

It was the day before Thanksgiving, and although she initially didn't think she wanted to go, Selena couldn't wait to board the plane later on. After four days of back and forth issues with Sean, she was exhausted. She stayed the first two nights at Tamara's house, but knew she had to face him and their reality at some point. The two days that they slept in the same bed were awkward. There was so much space between them, that a whole other person could have fit. Every time they tried to talk, it ended up in a screaming match. She didn't think she had any tears left. She hadn't eaten properly, and she was actually going to the salon wearing sweat suits.

Selena knew it was over between her and Sean. She told him that when she got back from Jamaica, they would sit and discuss their future living arrangements since they owned the house together. Sean reluctantly agreed.

Selena closed the salon early. She had just gotten a manicure and pedicure, and now was on her way to meet Tamara at her house. She was excited about going to sip tropical drinks on the beach with her sister. As much as she hated to admit it, she missed Sean. She tried to think of any excuse to give their relationship another chance. Unfortunately, every time she thought she had it figured out, the thought of Sean feeding a newborn that she did not give birth to, made her realize she could not do it.

She pulled up to Tamara's house as her niece, Arielle, was hopping into her father's shiny blue Chevy Tahoe. She honked the horn to get their attention so she could give her only niece a hug before she departed. Arielle heard the horn and jumped down from the SUV, all decked out in her bright pink Juicy Couture sweat suit, her favorite pair of UGG boots, and extra glossy lips. Arielle was a beautiful mix of her mother and father. She had her father's chocolate complexion, with all of her mother's small facial features. She was tall and lean and always reminded Selena of a model. Her long jet-black hair was pulled back into a ponytail that swung from side to side as she walked down the driveway to see her aunt.

"Hey baby girl! How are you?"

"I'm fine, Aunt Leeni. Will you bring me something nice back from Jamaica?"

"Sheesh, no 'I'll miss you', 'have a safe flight', nothing?" She laughed.

"Yeah, all of that stuff. Just playing, I love you, and I will miss you… and still bring me something back."

They both burst out into laughter and hugged before Selena walked Arielle up to her father's truck. Selena spoke to Arielle's father and watched them back out of the driveway.

When she walked in, she could smell Tamara's Lolita Lempicka perfume, a fragrance that she personally could not stand. Two things that Selena loved were food and perfume. She could identify any perfume from a simple sniff. She yelled up to let Tamara know that she was in the house, but she could not hear her over the loud music.

Tamara was upstairs in her bedroom packing and dancing around to Keri Hilson's song "Turning Me On." She was startled when she turned and saw Selena standing there. "Girl! Let a bitch know when you are in their house!"

"I did, but you were so busy up here dancing around and spraying that stinkin' ass perfume to hear me. How come you're still packing? You are so last minute. We're going to miss the plane. Always —"

Tamara cut her off before she could finish. "Leen, please, we aren't gonna miss the plane. I plugged my curling irons up already. Can you pin curl me please, baby sis?"

Selena rolled her eyes and snatched a comb out of Tamara's hand before advising her to sit down.

It only took Selena twenty minutes to pin curl her sister's long locks. She was known for her speed when styling hair. Tamara stood up and gave herself a once over in her full-length mirror, admiring her beauty. She was tall, with long, full black hair. Her skin was a smooth caramel color, and she had a full figure that men in her life often compared to Beyoncé.

Selena stared at her sister and could not help but feel a little insecure. Not that she wasn't equally as gorgeous, but she had always admired Tamara's height and curves. Over the past few days since the Sean revelation, she had begun to doubt if she was beautiful enough. Selena was shorter than her sister and was a light brown complexion. She had worn her naturally light brown hair in a perfect bob since she was about 20 years old. Selena had curves as well as her sister, but she had more of a muscular build. There wasn't an ounce of fat on her frame. She had naturally curly hair that she never liked, so she always wore it bone straight. Most people never knew from looking at the pair that they were even related, let alone sisters.

The story was that Tamara was the spitting image of their father, and Selena of their mother. There were no pictures of either parent, so the girls never knew how true the statement was. Their maternal grandmother, Adelle Nichols, raised them. Their mother died of a brain aneurysm two months after giving birth to Selena, and their father had been in jail serving a life sentence for murder since their mother was five months pregnant with Selena. Their grandmother never took them to the prison to see their father, and when they become of age, they had no interest in locating or visiting him. They were perfectly happy with life the way it was.

Tamara had ordered a car service to take them to the airport. As soon as she put her last item in the bag, the doorbell rang. The thirty-minute ride to the airport was full of conversation about everything from clothes to ex-boyfriends. Once they arrived, they had enough time to grab a Cinnamon Sugar Pretzel from Auntie Anne's Pretzels, then board their three-hour flight to Montego Bay, Jamaica. The sisters were both exhausted and slept the entire flight. They didn't wake until the plane started to descend.

It was sunny and warm in Jamaica, and all Selena could think of was the beach and a tropical drink. They hurried to their hotel room to shower and get into their swimsuits. Selena was the first one out of the shower. She quickly dried off and moisturized her body with Juicy Couture body lotion. She pulled the front of her golden bronze tresses up, left a few strands hanging on the sides, and slipped into her orange, two-piece Victoria's Secret bathing suit.

Her body was tight, arm muscles, abs of steel, and legs of a cross-country runner. Her gold heart belly button ring dangled as she turned in the mirror to get the full 360 degree look at herself. She grabbed her favorite M·A·C lip-gloss and dabbed some bronzer on her face. She looked like a natural beauty. She yelled for Tamara to hurry up. She could smell the Caribbean food and was starving.

In a few minutes, the bathroom door opened and Tamara was standing there fully figured in a white, two-piece Marc Jacobs bathing suit. Her face was made up in beautiful shades of pink, with matching pink nails and toes, and a stylish pair of pink sunglasses.

The stunning pair made their way to the beach where they immediately laid out and ordered curried shrimp shish kabobs and Piña Coladas. There were plenty of beautiful females on the beach; however, with Selena's radiant smile and Tamara's aura of confidence, they were definitely catching the attention of the men.

Selena would always act as if she didn't notice, but Tamara would play into it, using her seductive personality to get an array of fruits, appetizers, and drinks sent over. Before they had their first Piña Colada and shish kabob, they had received a bottle of wine, fresh mango, and another order of the perfectly seasoned kabobs. Two handsome men were the reason for the tasty treats, and had finally gotten the nerve to approach the ladies. Selena noticed first and was a little bit irritated.

"Damn! Here the hell they come. T, I don't feel like all this chit chattin'. We haven't even been here 2 hours," she whined.

"Girl, please! Live a little, and not to mention, they both fine as hell. I'll let you pick which one you want," laughed

Tamara.

Selena couldn't help but laugh at her sister. She laughed so hard that she spilled her Piña Colada all over her perfectly toned legs.

"Let me get that for you," spoke the taller, darker fella who approached.

Before Selena could turn him down, he had grabbed a towel and begun to gently wipe her leg off. Selena smelled his scent and knew immediately that it was Burberry Touch, one of Sean's favorite colognes.

She grabbed the towel from the gentleman and stated rather harshly, "I have it."

The shorter of the two men began the introductions. He complimented both women on their beauty, but made it clear in so many words, that he was interested in Tamara. The two were frat brothers from college on their annual getaway. Chris, the chatty frat brother, did most of the talking as Tamara laughed at all of his corny jokes. Lorenzo, the other brother, sat uncomfortably. He didn't know how to re-approach Selena, who was staring off into space thinking of Sean as The Burberry Touch lingered in the air.

Tamara announced that she and Chris were going to sit at the bar and have cocktails. Selena was instantly irritated. She knew her sister. This was a tactic to try to get her to talk to Lorenzo. Selena tried to ignore him, but she had to admit, he was one handsome man. He was every bit of 6'1' with the smoothest dark skin. He was in shape, and had the most beautiful smile. His almond shaped eyes were exquisite, not only because of the shape, but because Selena had never seen such a dark complexioned person with eyes so light brown. She decided to at least indulge in the conversation. He had a great sense of humor, he smelled good, and the baritone of his voice made Selena melt. She was definitely attracted to him. She would be lying though, if she said that she could get Sean off her mind.

Although he had betrayed her, she loved him and was thinking of him. What was he doing? Was he with Nadiyah? Was he thinking of her? Her thoughts halted as Lorenzo touched her hand and asked her if she wanted another drink. Selena nodded her head yes and watched as Lorenzo walked off towards the bar.

He arrived back to Selena's chair shortly with yet another Piña Colada.

They talked for about an hour. It was long enough for Selena to find out that he was a thirty-four year old lawyer, who lived in New York City. It was also long enough for her to realize that she was on a vacation, and that Sean and his messy situation would be in Philly when she got back. She decided to let go and enjoy these four days of relaxation. Besides, Lorenzo was eye candy, successful, and very attentive. They lay on the beach until sunset, chatting about everything from music to politics.

Selena sat up and wrapped her arms around her knees. "Can I ask you a question?"

"Shoot!" Lorenzo responded.

She hesitated, and then in a soft whisper, she began to speak. "If a person truly loves someone, what makes them hurt that person?"

"I truly believe in making mistakes. Don't get me wrong, there are some people out here that continuously hurt the one they say they love, and those people are simply users. But for the ones that have made a mistake,

I don't think it's intentional. It's just that some mistakes have heavy consequences. Why do you ask? Have you been hurt?"

"Maybe, but I don't wanna talk about it. We're here to have fun, right?"

She quickly changed the mood of the conversation because she felt like tears were about to start falling as she thought of Sean.

"You're right about that, beautiful. Now can I ask you a question?"

"I'm listening."

"Do you like massages?"

"I thought you'd never ask," said Selena in an unusually sexy voice. The Piña Coladas had begun to kick in, and Selena was feeling very comfortable with the thought of Lorenzo rubbing and caressing her body.

Lorenzo stood up and reached for Selena's hand. She stood and allowed him to lead her down the beach to the villa where he was staying. Selena knew she wanted to have sex with Lorenzo, but she had not been with anyone other than Sean in six years, and she was nervous. She had never been a promiscuous woman, and if she did have sex with him, this would be the first time she had ever had sex with a man on the night she met him.

Lorenzo lifted Selena's chin and kissed her lips gently. Selena closed her eyes and enjoyed every second of the passionate kiss. He then took his strong hands and grabbed Selena's toned butt. He pressed her body closer to his. She loved the aggressiveness he showed while remaining tender at the same time. He nibbled down her neck, while his hands traveled up to her bikini top and untied it. In a matter of seconds, her size 34C breasts were exposed. Her nipples were at attention, and Selena began to caress Lorenzo's back.

She pushed him until he fell backwards on the bed, then climbed on top of him. He slid his swim trunks off and began to rub his hand up and down his very erect manhood. Selena replaced his hand with her own, and examined his rock hard member while she slowly caressed it. He was of average size, but smooth and all one color. She loved how he wasn't afraid to please himself in front of her.

He reached up and helped her take off her bikini bottoms before he reached over to pull a condom out the nightstand. Once it was on, he placed Selena on her stomach and entered her from behind. His moans turned Selena on even more. She yelled for him to fuck her harder as she looked back into his caramel-colored eyes. The sweat dripped from his chest as he gently grabbed Selena's hair and began to wildly kiss her neck. Their moans grew louder.

Lorenzo pulled himself out of Selena and quickly turned her on her back. He climbed on top of her and was back inside, quickly. She pushed his head down to her breasts, and he began to suck her nipples. Before long, Lorenzo let out a loud moan and thrust himself deeper inside of Selena. She knew he had reached his climax.

He slowly pulled out of Selena and dropped to his knees. He licked her from her belly button down to her clitoris. He sucked and kissed her pussy while she rubbed his head and shoulders. In a matter of minutes, Selena's legs began to quiver. She grabbed the back of his neck tightly and squeezed her legs around his back. Her juices covered Lorenzo's face.

They laid in the bed silently for almost twenty minutes before Lorenzo asked, "Are you okay, Selena?"

"Yeah I'm fine. I need to get going, though."

"Really? You sure you don't just wanna stay?" he asked, sounding very confused.

"Yeah. We can maybe have lunch or something tomorrow, but I need to go."

Selena got up, put her bathing suit back on, and waited for Lorenzo to walk her across the beach to her hotel. The walk was very quiet and awkward. When Lorenzo tried to kiss her goodnight on the lips, she abruptly moved. Lorenzo automatically thought he hadn't performed well and felt embarrassed as he walked back to the villa. Selena walked into the hotel room and turned the light on to find Tamara asleep on the bed. She woke up when Selena shut the door.

"Well, where did you disappear to?" she grumbled in a half-asleep voice.

"You don't wanna know."

"If I didn't wanna know, I wouldn't have asked. Now stop playing, what's wrong?" Tamara snapped.

Selena plopped down on the bed, leaned back, and let out a huge sigh. Tamara got up and went to lay next to her sister.

"What's wrong, lil' sis? You're thinking about Sean, huh?"

Selena didn't answer. When Tamara looked over, Selena had tears flowing back to her ears.

She took a deep breath and started to speak softly. "I had sex with Lorenzo."

Tamara sat straight up and asked with serious concern, "You wanted to, right? He didn't—"

Selena cut her off and gave a small smile. "No, it was totally consensual. He didn't rape me."

Tamara was relieved to know that she didn't have to catch a homicide case in Jamaica. She was always the protector of her little sister, and would die herself before she allowed someone to hurt her.

"Well what's wrong, Leeni?"

Selena explained that even though she enjoyed every minute of what had just happened between her and Lorenzo, she felt guilty, as if she had betrayed Sean. Her sister assured her that it was a normal feeling for any decent woman. She also reminded her of the hurt that Sean has made her endure, and that it was just fine to experience some pleasure. Tamara wanted every steamy detail of the sexcapade. She jumped up and brewed some chamomile tea. The two sat up for hours talking, sipping tea, laughing and enjoying each other's company. Selena was beginning to feel a whole lot better.

The pair didn't awake until after noon due to their much-needed girl time in the wee hours of the morning. They showered and dressed then headed down to the hotel lobby for their all-inclusive lunch. Selena snacked on pieces of fruit and fresh mango juice while Tamara indulged in porridge with fresh cinnamon and a cold glass of coconut water.

As they finished their lunch, Selena noticed Lorenzo and Chris standing by the pool speaking with what appeared to be some of their fraternity brothers. They made eye contact, but Lorenzo quickly turned away. Selena knew that he felt uncomfortable because of the way she acted after they had sex the night before. She wanted to let him know that she was sorry, and that she had enjoyed their evening. She excused herself from the table with Tamara who had already begun talking to someone about the hotel's color schemes. Tamara had no problem promoting her interior design company, and was always successful in obtaining new clients.

Selena stood by the bar about ten feet from where the guys were standing. She was trying to catch Lorenzo's eye again. It took all of about three minutes before he noticed her standing there in a pair of short jean shorts, pink diesel tank top, and pink thong flip-flops. He couldn't help but notice her petite, athletic stature. He was instantly turned on at the fact that she had perfectly round breasts that sat up beautifully in her tank top without a bra. She had washed her hair in the shower and decided to wear it naturally curly. She had on just a touch of makeup.

She summoned him to come over, and he obliged. They greeted each other with a hug as he complimented her on her perfume. She thanked him and informed him that it was a fragrance named Creed. Selena got right to her apology and even explained why she felt that way afterwards. She talked briefly about how Sean had broken her heart and asked if Lorenzo would forgive her behavior.

He gave her a huge, warm hug that made Selena smile from ear to ear, and answered in just four words. "Of course I will."

He walked back over to his frat brothers, high-fived and hugged them, then returned to where Selena was standing. He escorted her back to the table where Tamara sat.

Lorenzo and Tamara greeted each other with a hug and the three sat and became more acquainted.

Tamara was always the more comedic of the sisters,

and Lorenzo barely stopped laughing, as she explained why she was not interested in his friend.

"No disrespect, he is a nice guy, but he's just not my type. He is a little too obnoxious for my liking. I prefer more quiet, laid-back brothers, and not to mention he had the most horrible breath last night."

Lorenzo was so caught so off guard by her comments that he nearly choked on his beverage. The three laughed for what seemed like forever. Tamara excused herself from the table and decided to go to the beach, listen to the live calypso band, and indulge in tropical drinks while her sister enjoyed the company of Lorenzo. Tamara's main objective for this trip was to keep her sister's mind off Sean. Judging by the smile on her face, it was working.

Selena and Lorenzo sat at the table for hours, drinking, talking, and of course enjoying the delicious tastes of the island foods. They vowed to keep in contact once they left the island, since they were only two hours away from each other. Selena realized that as much as she was enjoying his company, their time would be over soon, until whenever the two of them had enough free time to meet up back home. Lorenzo was set to leave, and Selena knew that once she was back at home, the reality of having to deal with the "Sean situation" would be right back in effect.

She decided to live a little on the adventurous side, even if it was only for one more night. She stood up and danced seductively over to the side of the table where Lorenzo was sitting. The sounds of the band and the smell of good food were in the air. She reached for his hand as he stood up and pulled her closer to him. They held each other tightly and began to kiss deeply. Selena could feel the stiffness of Lorenzo's manhood against her body and reached up so she could whisper in his ear that she wanted him.

Lorenzo picked Selena up and carried her down the beach as far as they could go until they were secluded. They lay on the beach sweaty and satisfied, Selena without a care in the world. She felt good, and promised herself from that night on that she would love herself first, and enjoy life.

The ladies saw Lorenzo and Chris off the next evening. Selena didn't feel as sad as she thought she would, probably because she knew that she and Lorenzo would see each other again. She could be spontaneous with him, and that felt good to her. Tamara felt like partying and wanted to go a reggae club in town. Selena, who usually had inhibitions about everything, was ready for action. They had two days left in Jamaica, and she wanted to enjoy every minute of it.

Tamara was dressed first. She pulled her long hair up into a neat bun because she knew it would be hot in the club, and she intended to dance the night away. She had on a hot pink mini-dress with a plunging back line. She was adorned in all silver accessories and a pair of silver rhinestone stiletto sandals. The hot pink lipstick on her caramel skin was gorgeous. Two sprays of Gucci Rush later, Selena emerged, showing off what she proclaimed to be her best physical feature, her breasts, in a red and black strapless dress. The top portion was a black tube dress, and the bottom portion was tiered black and red. The all-black wedge heel shoe paired with the dress made her look curvier than usual, and she was still rocking the naturally curly look in her bronze hair.

They caught a cab to the club, and from the moment

they walked in, they knew this would go down in the memory books as one of those nights to remember.

The club called The Jungle was jam packed with wall to wall people, loud music, smoke of every kind, and hot, sweaty bodies grinding on one another. Selena was amazed at how well the native Jamaican women moved their bodies. She was a good dancer, but she knew she had nothing on them. Tamara could never dance, but you couldn't tell her that. Offbeat and all over the place, she was always the life of the party.

They made their way to the bar and ordered two shots of Patron, then hit the dance floor. Two men immediately joined in with the sisters, and they danced seductively. Song after song, they grinded, jumped, and enjoyed the night. After about forty-five minutes of non-stop dancing, they decided to make their way to the bathroom. Those plans were quickly halted. They had no idea that anyone was even performing at the club that night, and halfway to the bathroom, reggae artist Movado made his way to the stage. There was no possible way they could make it now.

They stood and rocked with the rest of the crowd as he began to sing one of his more popular songs. The crowd chanted and sang along, "Money don't change we, we are money changers..."

After he had performed three songs, he exited the stage with about four Jamaican women he had picked from the audience to dance on stage with him. Once they got to the bathroom, they joked about how Movado and the ladies were about to have a great night. Both of the ladies were feeling very "irie" as the natives said. They had been drinking all night and had smoked some of the "other" type of cigarettes as they were being passed through the club.

Tamara went into the stall while Selena stood at the sink wiping her sweaty face down. She pulled her cell phone out of her red clutch bag to check the time, only to notice that she had seven missed calls and three text messages. She couldn't understand why she had so many. She didn't even socialize with many people, and the closest person in her life was with her. The last missed call was from Lorenzo. She smiled because he had followed her directions. She told him to call when he arrived safely back in New York, so that had to be what he wanted to tell her.

She moved to her text messages before even glancing at the other missed calls. She wanted to text Lorenzo and let him know that she was sorry she missed his call, and that she would call in the morning. She was shocked to see three texts from Danielle, the makeup artist who worked in her shop, saying to call her, and it was an emergency. The next text was from Sean's sister Marissa. The text was in all capital letters. *SEAN HAS BEEN SHOT. HE NEEDS YOU.*

Selena went back to her call log and noticed that the other six missed calls were from Danielle, Marissa, and Sean's mom, Ms. Gladys. She felt weak and threw up right in the sink. Tamara made her way out of the bathroom, clueless as to what was going on.

Selena began to yell. "I need to get the hell out of here! He needs me."

She cried uncontrollably while her sister shook her and repeatedly asked what was wrong. Selena suddenly blacked out, and her limp body dropped to the bathroom floor. Tamara fell to her knees, lifted her sister's head, and began to yell for help.

* * * * *

Selena lay in a hospital bed, finally awake and sipping on ginger ale. Her thoughts were scattered, and she wanted to go home. She needed to see Sean. Maybe this was a sign that she needed to try to make things right with him. She was hurt and confused, but she loved and missed him. The tears rolled uncontrollably down her face. She asked for Tamara, who sat in the waiting room.

Tamara had Selena's phone, and was finally able to put the pieces together regarding what happened with Sean. She was able to speak with Danielle and find out that Sean fought as long as could, but the bullet wound to the head had claimed his life.

He was on a routine traffic stop in the 22nd district. The driver of the car was notified that not only was his license suspended, but that there was an outstanding warrant for his arrest. The driver was asked to step out of his vehicle by Officer Sean Miller, and when he did, he pulled out a .45 caliber pistol and shot him two times–once in the head, and once in the abdomen.

Tamara wanted to see her sister, who had suffered an anxiety attack after she received the text, but dreaded having to tell her that Sean didn't make it. Although Tamara despised Sean for what he had done to her sister, she knew that Selena loved this man. They most likely would've worked their relationship out at some point. The thought was now impossible.

As soon as Tamara walked in the room, her tears immediately began to fall. Even with her hair all over her head and mascara lines on her face, Selena still looked beautiful to Tamara. She had a flashback of their grandmother bringing this newborn baby into the living room of their Southwest Philadelphia row home 31 years ago. Tamara was five years old. She sat on the plastic covered couch with her arms out to hold the new baby. She held her and looked at her precious face as only a big sister could. This was the same face that, in their lifetime, Tamara had to explain the most complicated issues; from their mother's death, to their father's incarceration, to boys and sex, and now this. The love of her life, murdered at the age of 33. She walked over to her sister, kissed her forehead, and grabbed her hand tightly. She took her other hand and caressed her sister's face.

"I'm okay, T. Were you able to talk to Ms. Gladys or anyone? How is Sean?" she asked in desperation.

Tamara put her head down and spoke gently. "He didn't make it, Leeni, I'm sorry."

Selena began to yell. "Speak up, I can't hear you. Where is Sean?" she demanded.

Just then, a nurse ran into the room to see what all of the noise was about. When she came in, Tamara was trying to hold and calm Selena, but she screamed, kicked and cried uncontrollably. Two more nurses ran in, and they were finally able to restrain her. They administered a sedative that made her relax and calm down.

Tamara was asked to leave the room to let Selena get some rest. Although physically she was fine, suffering from an anxiety attack and adding more stress and excitement could easily lead to more serious issues. After two hours of waiting in the hospital, making more calls regarding Sean, and checking in on her daughter, Arielle, a nurse finally came over to Tamara and said that they were in the process of discharging her sister.

After about five minutes, she was wheeled out of the room. Tamara fought back tears as she tried to imagine the pain her sister was feeling. Selena's eyes were puffy and red, with dark circles surrounding them. Her skin was paler than it had ever been, and although they had only been in the hospital for about 7 hours, she looked like she had lost weight. They wheeled her curbside of the hospital exit, and the pair got in a cab and rode in complete silence the entire twenty-minute ride to the hotel.

Once they arrived back, Selena immediately got in the shower. The bathroom was steaming hot, and she stayed in there for almost a half hour. What seemed like her entire relationship with Sean flashed through her head as the hot water rolled down her body. She sobbed silently as she thought of the moment she met Sean at the supermarket, down to their fight last week about his unborn child. She turned off the water and grabbed a towel. She stood in front of the full-length bathroom mirror and brushed her wet, curly hair back into a ponytail. She brushed her teeth and walked out into the room where Tamara sat quietly on the bed.

"Leeni, I'm so sorry for your loss. I'm here for you, talk to me."

"I don't wanna talk, T. Had it not been for the bright idea to come here, Sean may still be living!" she yelled.

"Oh, so it's my fault? He was a fuckin' cop, Leen! This shit could have happened whether you were home or not! I brought you here to clear your mind because he did you wrong, did you forget?" she snapped.

Selena became enraged. "So that's more important than his life, huh? That's real fucked up, T!"

She grabbed her suitcase and began to toss all of her

belongings in it. Once she was done, she told Tamara that she needed to get to the airport.

CHAPTER 3

They arrived at Philadelphia International at about four in the afternoon. Tamara hopped in the car service and asked her sister if she was getting in. She received no answer. She waited a couple of minutes before she told the driver to pull off.

Selena waited until she had pulled off before she waved down a cab. She silently cried the entire ride home. Pulling into the driveway of the town home that she shared with Sean, knowing that he was no longer there, felt surreal. Someone had left an enormous bouquet of flowers at the front door, which made Selena realize that he was really gone forever.

She paid the cab driver and walked slowly to the door. She turned her key and walked into the foyer. She walked up the stairs to their bathroom and smiled as she saw Sean's underwear still on the bathroom floor. Any other day, she would have complained, but today it didn't matter. She picked up the shirt and began to rub it on her face. She inhaled the fresh clean smell of Burberry Touch that was all over his shirt. She ran to their bedroom and began to scream and throw everything around. Clothes, perfumes, even the flat screen TV all flew around the room. She felt hurt, guilty, and alone.

She thought that his family would never forgive her for not being there for him. While she was away being a whore, her love was losing his life. Images of Nadiyah raced through her head. She wondered if she had been to their home while she was away. Was the baby she carried even Sean's? Did his family know about her? She decided to pull herself together and go face what she could not avoid. She knew they would be planning his funeral, and she wanted to be a part of it. She changed into her all-black BCBG sweat suit and a pair of UGGs. She got in her car and drove to his mother's house.

There wasn't any parking on Wagner St., that day. Selena almost forgot that Sean was a police officer, and his death would be all over television. There were police cars, television station vans, and what looked like the entire family's cars lining the street. She finally reached the front door of his mother's home and waited nervously for someone to answer. She didn't recognize the person that answered the door, but there were a lot of unfamiliar faces in the usually quiet home.

She finally spotted Marissa, Sean's sister, and the two embraced. The tears began to fall again as Marissa recounted the events that led to his death. Marissa walked Selena to the back of the house and down to the finished basement where Ms. Gladys sat on a chair speaking to someone whose back was turned to Selena and Marissa. Selena made her way over to Ms. Gladys and hugged her as she whispered numerous times in her ear, "I'm so sorry."

Once they finished embracing, Selena's tears turned to anger as she turned around and saw that the person Ms. Gladys was speaking with was Nadiyah. Her heart dropped and her legs felt numb. She knew it wasn't the time or place, but she couldn't help but ask Nadiyah what she was doing there.

Nadiyah looked up and stared at Selena with her green eyes and answered, "I'm here because my daughter's father was murdered. I have every right to be here. I should be asking you what you are doing here. Didn't you give Sean his ring back? Which means you were no longer his fiancé."

Ms. Gladys quickly put an end to what was about to happen. She let them know that her son was her main concern, and that she wasn't about to let the two of them argue and fight in her house about her son. Ms. Gladys was a sweetheart, and she adored Selena, but Sean was her only son and a momma's boy. Selena knew that whatever was going on with Nadiyah, she knew about it.

Without another word, Selena walked upstairs and then out the front door. She pulled out her iPhone, ready to call Tamara. Instead, she opted to text her, remembering their argument at the hotel and the silence on the plane ride home. Selena was upset with Tamara, but she was her best friend and the only person who could make her feel better about what was going on. She touched the letters on her phone quickly and sent a message that read: I NEED YOU.

Tamara called instead of texting.

"Where are you?"

"I'm sorry, T, for earlier and—"

Tamara quickly cut her off and told her that there was no need for all of that. She simply wanted to know what was wrong and where she was. Selena told her that she was at Sean's mom's house, but she was leaving and that she would meet her at the Melrose Diner on Broad Street.

Tamara agreed and was on her way within minutes.

By the time Tamara arrived, Selena was already there eating a slice of cheesecake with a huge pair of Christian Dior sunglasses on. Her hair was limp, and not even a dab of gloss had graced her cracked lips. Tamara walked over, sat down in front of her sister, and reached for her hands across the table. Selena put her fork down and grasped her sister's hands tightly.

"What happened?" Tamara asked.

"I just feel so stupid and used. I feel bad because I'm snapping at you, thinking of my own feelings, and this man…this man I was about to marry is gone forever. I don't know whether to be mourning his death or beginning a new chapter in my life. After all the lies and deceit, it hurts so badly. She was there with his family, with Marissa's niece and Ms. Gladys' grandchild in her stomach. I show up, and I'm nothing. He told them that I gave him the ring back. She looked at me like I was nothing."

Tamara cried. She felt her sister's pain. She was nearly at a loss for words, but as usual, she found the perfect thing to say. It made sense, and most importantly, made Selena feel better.

"Leeni, listen, I cannot act like I know how it feels, because I don't. But you asked should you be mourning his death, or starting a new chapter. BOTH! The answer is both. It is fine to mourn him. You loved him, and regardless of the revelations about the baby, you know Sean loved you. He was human and made mistakes. At the same time, you will also need to move forward. It's gonna take time, and it's not going to be easy, but you are strong. We've been through some shit in our lifetime, and you know this. You have me and Ari. I'm never gonna see you fail. You can cry, scream, do whatever you need to do. I'm here for you. I love you."

Tamara signaled the waitress for the check, and the two got into their separate cars and drove to Tamara's home. When they arrived, Ari was there with her best friend Kierra. The girls were in the kitchen eating pizza, texting, and giggling all at the same time. They barely paid any mind to Selena and Tamara as they offered subtle "Heys" between bites of pizza and texts. Selena walked over and grabbed her niece's face as she always did and kissed her forehead.

She smiled and whined, "Aunt Leeni!"

"Aunt Leeni, what? I know you are not acting shy in front of Kierra Bear. She has been around long enough to know she's next."

She turned quickly and made the same affectionate gesture to Kierra.

Tamara grabbed a slice of pizza and made her way down to the basement. Selena poured a glass of ruby red grapefruit juice and followed behind her sister.

Tamara had lived in her home for almost eight years, and Selena was always amazed at how she was constantly doing new and creative things to reinvent her space. Tamara got bored with things quickly, from furniture to vehicles, even men. The only staples that have ever remained constant in her life were Selena and Arielle.

The brick fireplace looked beautiful, and had the basement just the right temperature. The furniture was a deep mahogany brown, soft Italian leather with cream faux-fur throw pillows adorning it. The floors were hardwood, but had the same cream-colored fur throw rugs in various locations. The 52-inch plasma TV made the basement look like a modern day cabin, and Selena could not wait to relax.

Tamara walked over to her cherry wood bar and poured them both a glass of her favorite wine, Moscato. They sat and talked about Sean's death and helping Selena get through it. Selena was very emotional when talking about the funeral. She even thought badly of herself for being concerned with seeing Nadiyah there and wondering how many people actually knew about Sean's infidelity versus actually being upset that Sean was deceased.

Tamara assured her that she would feel plenty of emotions, and to not down herself for being human. The funeral was in just three days, and Selena wondered how she would ever recover from this. Besides her phone ringing constantly, it was a constant reminder of the hurt to see Sean's face all over the TV and on the front page of the Daily News. He was the third officer killed in the line of duty that year alone in Philadelphia.

* * * * *

The night before the funeral, as Selena stood in her bedroom wrapping her hair for bed, she watched the ten o'clock news. They of course spoke of Sean's murder, the arrangements for the funeral service, and of a fund that had been set up at PNC Bank for his unborn daughter. Selena snatched her remote control from her vanity and turned the television off. She held back the tears as she lay across her bed–the bed that still held the scent of Sean's colognes. It wasn't long before she fell off into a deep sleep.

Selena woke up at six the next morning to a call from her sister. She assured her that she was up and would be ready when she and Arielle arrived at eight. Selena stood in her steaming hot shower, thinking of the times she and Sean spent making love there. She smiled as the water ran down her skin. The smile soon turned to tears as she realized that she would never be able to hold him again. She was also upset because since she had left Ms. Gladys' home three days ago, she had not heard from her, Marissa, or anyone from his family. That made it easier to believe that they knew all about Nadiyah and the baby. She felt hurt and betrayed, but vowed that she would hold it together today, and would be ready to begin a new chapter in her life tomorrow. She wouldn't worry about anyone from the past.

She moisturized her skin with Warm Vanilla Sugar by Bath and Body Works and sprayed herself with Narciso Rodriguez for Her. The two scents always complimented each other, especially in winter. She opted to wear a black, two-piece skirt suit with a dark gray satin David Meister Blouse. She chose a simple black round toe heel to wear. Her makeup was subtle; mascara, eyeliner, a hint of blush, and a light pink gloss on her perfectly pouty lips. She stood in her full-length mirror and looked at herself from every angle. At that moment, she realized that she did not have on her two-carat, princess cut engagement ring.

Her Blackberry rang as she headed over to her jewelry box to grab the ring. It was Tamara on the line letting her know that she was outside. Selena slid the beautiful ring on her finger, only to stare at it for a few seconds and remove it. She wiped a single tear from her eye as she walked down the steps and grabbed her mink coat that Sean had just gotten out of storage for the season a few short weeks ago. She then walked out the front door to join Tamara and Arielle.

The service lasted the entire morning and afternoon, from the viewing, to the police escorting Sean's body to the service, to the mayor and chief of police speaking. There were thousands of people on board to witness the locally televised event. Selena felt of no importance. Although she knew it was Sean's home going service, she was barely recognized by anyone, not even his family. Nadiyah, belly in tow, was the center of all attention. Members of the police force, his family, everyone made sure they hugged and comforted the woman who had just surfaced in Selena's life three weeks ago.

It appeared that everyone else knew exactly who she was, and if they didn't, they sure played a very good role in making the pregnant homewrecker feel loved. Selena was emotionally drained by the day's events, and decided not to go back to Ms. Gladys' house for the repast. She did not feel welcomed, and wanted the day to be over. She had Tamara wait with her in the car at the burial site until everyone left so that she could speak with Sean alone.

She stood next to his gravesite and threw one single red rose over the dirt. She began to cry as she spoke to Sean as if he were standing right there. She told him that she loved him and always would, but not even his death would let her forget what he had done to her.

"You broke our bond, the one we said no one would ever be able to break. I trusted you, and I gave you my all. Know that you were the first and the last man to ever have that honor. I love you, Sean."

She turned and walked away, never once looking back at his grave.

CHAPTER 4

It had been four months since Sean's death, and life was pretty much back to normal. Selena had resumed her full-time schedule in the shop about a month ago, and her spirits were pretty good. It was April, the start of spring, Selena's favorite season. Mary J Blige's "What's the 411" CD was playing in the shop this particular Saturday. The windows were open, which allowed a warm breeze to flow through while the beautiful pink curtains fluttered about. Tamara was sitting in Selena's chair getting her hair pressed out bone straight for a lunch meeting that she had with a potential celebrity client. Arielle sat at the front desk as usual, reading one of her teen novels, and Danielle sat with a client discussing the latest makeup trends for a summer wedding.

Selena's next appointment wasn't until 1:00 p.m., and it was only 10 a.m. She was planning to go out, enjoy the weather, and ride over to Ridge Avenue to Johnny Manana's for lunch. Her absolute favorite food was Mexican, and they had the best chicken enchiladas. She was finished with Tamara's hair, and it looked fantastic. She never charged her sister or niece for services, but every time she so much as touched their hair, Tamara would leave money on her station. The money would usually go from the station to Selena's hand, and then be slipped into Arielle's pocket.

Tamara thanked her sister, grabbed her Louis Vuitton classic hobo bag, and scurried over to the desk where Ari sat and kissed her forehead. She looked up, smiled at her mother, and wished her good luck. Selena picked up the $50 her sister had left, walked over to her niece and slid it in the pocket of her jean shorts. She let Danielle know that she was about to step out for lunch, and asked if she and Ari wanted anything. They both said no, as they had already decided they were going to order Chinese.

Selena grabbed her keys, opened her sunroof and turned her radio up. Keri Hilson's "Knock you Down" was on and she tapped her fingers on the steering wheel to the beat. The wind felt great, blowing through her hair. She had decided to let it grow out of her normal bob haircut, and it was almost shoulder length. She had also colored her hair last week to a crimson color. She had gotten plenty of compliments since she had decided to make a drastic change to her hair. Her hair was naturally a light brown color. She had used bronze to color her hair since high school, so much that people thought it was her natural color. Something about the richness of the red brought out a different side of Selena. She looked sexier, more intriguing, and not so girl next door-ish.

She sat at a red light, staring at herself in her car mirror. She couldn't help but smile at herself. She liked the change. She was feeling her new aura. She was more carefree and laid-back over the last few months, as well. She still maintained her appearance, but her style was different. Instead of blouses and heeled shoes to work every day, she indulged in cute designer jeans and Chanel sneakers. This look was more youthful than her prior, stuffier look. She didn't look 32, and she sure didn't feel it.

She found a parking spot on the side of the restaurant and walked into Johnny Manana's and ordered her chicken enchiladas and fresh brewed iced tea. Selena couldn't help but notice the man that was staring at her while he sat at one of the tables. She was flattered, but had no real interest. She hadn't noticed anyone since Lorenzo in Jamaica, and she definitely wasn't interested in dating.

She hadn't answered any of Lorenzo's calls since the day after Sean's funeral when she explained to him what had happened. He began to text and call on an almost daily basis just a week after the funeral, and Selena simply wasn't ready to deal with him. He had stopped calling and texting over a month ago, and although Selena had thought of him, she was stubborn. She decided that she wasn't going to be the one to call.

Selena sat at a small table in the back of the restaurant, texting to see how things were going with Tamara's meeting. She noticed that the man who was initially staring at her, was now standing at her table. She tried to ignore him, but then he introduced himself. He was Paul Major, average height and olive complexioned. It was obvious that he was not all black, if any at all. There was nothing spectacular as far as physique, but he was gorgeous. He had dark, low cut hair that Selena could tell was naturally curly once grown out. He was well dressed in a navy blue suit, crisp white shirt, and a navy blue and silver striped tie.

He smelled delicious, and once he spoke to Selena, she blurted out, "Blue de Chanel."

"Excuse me?" Paul responded.

"Blue de Chanel, your cologne, correct?"

"Oh yes, wow that's impressive!" He reached out to grab Selena's hand. Before she extended it, she stated her name.

"Pleased to meet you Ms. Nichols, do you often eat lunch alone?"

"Sometimes" she responded with a slight smile.

"Well, hopefully, we can change that. Feel free to call me anytime, and enjoy your lunch."

He handed a business card to Selena as he turned and walked out of the restaurant. Selena would be lying if she said he hadn't sparked her interest. She glanced down at his business card, which stated that he was a real estate broker. She slipped his card in her purse, then enjoyed her enchilada and iced tea before heading back to the salon.

The rest of the afternoon was routine, with her remaining four appointments. She thought of Lorenzo, and even Paul while she styled. She knew that aside from his attractive face, he wasn't generally her type. He wasn't as tall as anyone she had ever dated, he didn't have the muscular body type she was usually attracted to, and his career as real estate broker had to be pretty boring, showing houses all day. Despite all of those issues, she was still intrigued by him. She just didn't know if she was ready to find out why just yet. It seemed too early to begin dating. She still felt guilty for sleeping with Lorenzo on her and Tamara's trip to Jamaica, so with Sean being dead only four months, how could she begin dating?

Her logic was foolish to most, especially her sister. The reason they had even gone to Jamaica, was because not only did he cheat, but he'd also impregnated another woman. The baby had been born on January 19, 2009.

She was now about three months old. Selena had never seen her, but had heard she was beautiful, which is what she'd expected. Sean was handsome, and not-for-nothing, Nadiyah was an attractive woman, as well. Although she had never seen her, she had made an anonymous deposit of $2,500.00 into the account set up for her at the bank. She felt that it was the right thing to do.

She was still mad that Nadiyah knew about her and Sean and continued to see him, but she was young, 22, and a college student at the University of Penn, studying law. She was from the North Philadelphia area of the city; the district Sean had worked in. She had nothing, and Sean won her over by buying her nice things and taking her places she had never been. Since his death, she was living in University City near her school, and the city was paying her rent and childcare expenses for their daughter, Miyani. Sean had actually shared with Nadiyah the name that they always said would be their daughter's name. Through it all, Selena knew the baby had nothing to do with her parents' deceit.

It was about 8 p.m., when Selena finally locked the last lock on the salon and was able to begin her journey home. She looked down at her phone before she pulled off, and noticed there were no missed calls or texts from anyone, not even her sister. That was rare; the pair normally talked or texted all day. She hadn't even returned her text from earlier, asking about her meeting. She decided to call Arielle.

Arielle answered on the third ring, in her cheerful voice. Selena smiled from ear to ear as she first asked her niece how she was doing, and then if she had spoken to her mother. She let her know that she was just relaxing at her dad's house and that she hadn't talked to her mom. That still wasn't out of the ordinary. Ari was a teenager, and Selena was shocked that she had answered the phone for her call.

Selena decided to stop by Tamara's house. She figured the meeting most likely turned into a dinner, but wanted to be sure. Tamara's vehicle wasn't in her driveway, so she used her key to go in and double check. Something just seemed very odd to her now. She opened the door, yelled up for Tamara, and got no response. She checked every room in the house, her bedroom being last. Selena lifted the light switch, and noticed that there were clothes all over her bed, which was strange enough, because T was a complete neat freak, whose home never had an item out of place.

As she looked at the outfit that lay across the bed, she realized it was the black skirt set that she was wearing to her meeting that afternoon. Selena began to feel nervous, and dialed Tamara's number. The phone was now going directly to voicemail, and Selena's thoughts were all over the place.

She paced around Tamara's room, waiting for her phone to ring and Tamara to pick up and say she was ok. She sat on the side of the bed and noticed a piece of mail on the nightstand. Selena picked up the envelope and examined it carefully. It was open, with the yellow notebook paper hanging half way out, and postmarked April 11, 2009. The handwriting was impeccable, and it was addressed to Tamara from a correctional facility inmate by the name of Carl Anderson.

Selena's stomach began to turn, and she felt warm all over. Tamara had received a letter from Carl, their father, the man who had been incarcerated since Selena was in the womb of their mother. He was a drug-addicted murderer who killed a man that he had tried to rob. Selena was confused. Why did Tamara even give this man her address? What could he possibly want? Selena knew he was probably begging for money. That's it! He had heard from someone that Tamara was doing well, and he wanted to ask for money. He had to ask Tamara because she was the only one who knew him outside of prison. Selena had never seen him in person and didn't care to.

Selena began to laugh aloud at the thought of Carl asking Tamara for anything, and the response he would get from her. Tamara was cutthroat and straight to the point. She would never send her hard-earned money to a man who cared about his addiction more than his family.

Selena opened the top nightstand drawer so that she could put the pathetic piece of mail away. Her chest tightened as she looked in the drawer. There were tons of letters from Carl, and even a notepad. Was Tamara responding to this junk mail? Why didn't she tell Selena that he was writing her? And why hadn't he ever tried to send a letter to her?

She knew it was wrong, but she began to read the letters. Every letter was the same where this man thanked Tamara for the money she had sent and pictures of his granddaughter, Arielle, and had confirmed a date of what appeared to be a monthly visit. Selena was enraged. How could she be sneaking around and going to visit this heartless man? Tamara was always the strong one. Why was she weak for this man she had not been around since she was five years old? He had no value to society; he was a crack addict and a two-time murderer. Not only had he killed the man he tried to rob, but the story was that he killed another man while in prison, which was the reason he received an additional 15-year sentence.

Selena picked up her phone to dial her sister again. It still went straight to voicemail, which made no sense because even if her phone had died, she always kept a car charger and a USB charger with her. Her emotions were all over the place. She was worried about her sister, upset that she had been keeping the letters from her, and enraged that she even wanted a relationship with him. The last letter that she read from the inmate at Coal Township Correctional facility confirmed everything for Selena. On this day, April 18, 2009, Carl Anderson, after spending 32 years in jail, would be released, and his "baby girl" would be picking him up.

Selena was numb, and her mind wandered. She had to go home and lie down. Her head was pounding, and no pain reliever would be able to help. She needed to cry, scream, and cry again until she fell off to sleep. She grabbed her keys and phone off the bed, turned the light down, and quickly ran out of the front door.

The tears flowed down her face as she drove in silence. She thought about her life, and how it has been filled with constant hurt and pain. The agony of growing up without a mother or father, the death of her grandmother, death of her fiancé, the child that her fiancé created with another woman, and now this; there were far more hurtful memories than happy ones in her opinion, and she was ready to be done with it all.

As she drove home on 76 Eastbound, her phone rang. It was none other than Tamara. On her first three calls, Selena pushed the "IGNORE" button. She had nothing to say to her, but by the fourth call, she decided to answer.

Tamara was her usual upbeat self, saying that her phone had died at the dinner, but she was pretty sure she had acquired the client. Selena couldn't believe the audacity of her sister to continue to lie, knowing she was with Carl today.

She could not take the story any longer and yelled, "Stop fuckin' lyin' to me, T! I know everything. I know about Carl. I know you know I have always been in contact with him. I know you were visiting him, sending him money, sending him pictures of Ari, and I know he was released today and that you were there waiting with open arms to get him. So where is he? Is he right there in the passenger side of your truck that you worked hard for? Did you give him more money yet? Huh, T?"

Selena went on for about 5 minutes before Tamara cut her off. She told her that she was sorry she had lied, and begged for her sister's forgiveness. She begged for Selena to meet up with her. She said she would be home in about a half hour and to just meet her there. Selena snapped, explaining that she had just left her home because she was worried about her and that she saw the letters from Carl.

"I'm sorry, Leeni. I swear I was going to tell you, but I knew you would be hurt. You have to understand, that is my dad, and although I was young, we had a relationship before he went to jail. It was a void in my life that I decided to fill about 8 years ago," Tamara explained.

"So you have been lying to me for 8 years, keeping in contact with this waste of a man, who has done nothing for us our entire lives?"

"That waste of a man is my father, and everyone makes mistakes. I have forgiven him, and I am ready to move past all the wrong he has done, and at least give him a chance." she said, full of passion.

"And you are right," Selena interjected. "You are a grown woman, and if you have decided to allow him into your life, that is your decision. Foolish as it may be, it is your decision. I never would've thought that you of all people would ever be so weak to believe the words of a crack addicted convicted felon. And to trust him with your heart, and not just your heart, your daughter's heart. You are pitiful Tamara. Be sure to tell Carl, that I, Selena Nichols, will never accept or forgive him," she stated cold-heartedly.

Selena's words were piercing and harsh, and Tamara began to cry. One thing she had always done was protect her younger sister, but she couldn't do it anymore. She knew at this very moment, that Selena needed to know the truth, no matter how much it hurt her.

"It wouldn't matter if you did or not, he has no interest in you forgiving him or being a part of his life."

"And you think I care? I'm glad he doesn't want a relationship with me. What does that matter to me at 32 years old? Why would I try to start a relationship with my father who's been in jail since my mother was pregnant with me?"

"He's not your father," whispered Tamara.

Selena was too busy ranting to even hear the words that her half-sister had spoken to her. She waited about thirty seconds and screamed at the top of her lungs into the phone.

"He's not your father!"

The phone was completely silent for almost two minutes before Selena spoke.

"What are you talking about, T? What the hell is going on?"

"Exactly what I said. Carl Anderson is not your father.

He's my father. He was never addicted to drugs. The man he killed was his friend Raymond Wilson, your REAL father. Our mother, the beloved woman that Grandma put on a pedestal while she dogged my father out, was a whore. She was sleeping with my father's friend Raymond, your father.

"My dad got laid off from work in the fall of 1977 and was on his way home earlier than usual. When he got there, our mother and your father were there in bed together. Mom and my father were already on the verge of divorce because of other affairs she had on him before, so when he walked in on them, he lost it. He began to choke Raymond, and before long, he passed out and died. She was already pregnant with you. Everyone knew it wasn't my dad's baby. He loved her and wanted it to work regardless, but after catching them in the act, it ruined any plans of being happily ever after."

Selena pulled her car over because she began to feel weak. How could her sister be speaking of their mother this way? This couldn't be true. She felt lost, angry, and confused all at once.

"Why are you doing this, T? What's wrong with you? Do you honestly believe the lies this man has told you?"

Tamara cut her off. "Listen here, Selena, it's the truth. Of course, Grandma would tell us that it was all my father's fault because Mom was her daughter. Listen, meet me at my house, we need to talk about this face-to-face," she begged.

"I don't wanna see you right now. Do you understand how I'm feeling? My whole fuckin' life has been a lie. My relationship with Sean a lie, you're a liar, my sister… Well yeah, my half-sister is a whole fuckin' liar!" she screamed.

"Alright, you know what, Leeni? Get the fuck over yourself. Every time in life that something has happened since I was five, I've had to sacrifice the truth because of you. Be there when you needed a shoulder to cry on, make sure you stayed out of trouble, and through all of this, I had to deal with how I felt about life and the circumstances that made it how it was, alone. So for once in your life, try and understand how I feel. The world does not revolve around you, Selena Ann Nichols."

"So wait a minute. The family comes up with the idea to lie to me about who I really am, and because you go along with it for 32 years when you could have told me this shit when we were teenagers, you feel some kinda way? Honestly, if I wouldn't have seen the letters, you would have never told me. When I made that vow as a teenager not to fuck with bitches, you should have been the first one on the list," she snapped.

"Bitch!? Yeah, you have lost your mind. You can call or come past when you are ready to talk like grown ass women, but you're not gonna disrespect me at all."

"Wait on that call, Tamara." Selena hung up the phone.

She sat in the Wal-Mart parking lot on Roosevelt Blvd and cried for almost an hour. She sat quietly and reflected on her childhood. It all made sense now. There were times as a child that Tamara would go spend the weekends at who she thought was her dad's family's house, and Grandma would never let Selena go. There was always an excuse. *Leeni you are too young, Tamara is older and can take care of herself over there.* By the time she got what was considered old enough, she had no interest in going, and Tamara didn't go much anymore either.

Selena was a mess. She had no idea who she really was. Her whole life was a lie. The things that people thought would protect her were now right in her face, haunting her. She loved her sister, but she knew it would be a long time before she forgave her.

CHAPTER 5

Almost a month had passed since Selena and Tamara had spoken. Selena was feeling depressed, not only because of her sister, but also because of her niece. Tamara had not allowed Arielle to come to the shop since everything happened. Once Tamara involved Arielle, Selena knew it was even more serious than she had imagined. There were so many nights that Selena wanted to call or stop by Tamara's home, but changed her mind. She didn't know if Carl was living with Tamara, or even if Tamara wanted to be bothered.

Selena realized that she was very harsh in their last conversation and that a lot was said out of anger. She owed Tamara an apology, and Tamara needed to explain Carl to her since her lies regarding to her contact with him had sparked the whole incident.

Selena picked up her phone to call Tamara, who answered on the second ring. She sounded either sleep or sick. The first few minutes of the conversation were to catch up on Arielle. Arielle had been her heart since she was born, and these past few months without her were emotional. Tamara transitioned to the meat and potatoes of the conversation by first apologizing.

"Listen, Leeni, me apologizing cannot change our

history. It is what it is. We are half-sisters. That means absolutely nothing to me though. I've loved you since you came home from the hospital, and no DNA could change that. I am sorry for continuing the lie for so long. Should I have told you? Of course. Did I know exactly what to say? No. I am sorry."

"T, thank you for apologizing and I would like to apologize for my reaction, but do you understand my feelings? I have no idea who I am. To hear at this age the truth about my parents when I had a whole different perception of both of them is devastating to me. I've lost Grandma, who apparently lied to me. Sean lied to me, and now he's gone. You lied to me. I feel so lost."

Tears dropped down Selena's face. Tamara was equally a wreck.

"Leeni, we need to get together. This is not a conversation that we need to have over the phone. Besides, there are a lot of other things going on that only you as my sister can help me get through. First and foremost, do you accept my apology?"

Selena accepted Tamara's apology, and they set a lunch date to sit and talk as sisters and iron out their differences. Although Selena felt better that she had talked to Tamara, she still felt empty. She knew it would take a lot of talking and understanding for her and Tamara to be as close as they had always been, but she was up for the challenge.

* * * * *

It was a beautiful Saturday evening in May, and Selena had just left the salon. She was ready to go home and relax. On the way there, her cell phone rang. It was Andrea, one of the few clients that Selena talked to outside of the salon. Selena was hesitant at first, because usually when Andrea called, it was to gossip, but she answered anyway.

"Hey girl, what you doin' tonight?" asked Andrea.

"Not a thing, but taking my behind home. I am tired."

"OMG, such an old lady. I thought you might want to go to Copa's and have a few drinks. It's really warm out tonight."

Selena actually thought it would be nice, tired and all. She hadn't been out since the club in Jamaica, and a tasty cocktail or two was all the persuasion she needed. She agreed to meet Andrea at her West Philly apartment in about two hours.

Selena showered and put on a pair of American Apparel black fitted leggings, a white tank top, and a pair of black and white BCBG peep toe pumps. Her hair was flowing. She smelled like she had just been sprayed out of the Emilio Pucci bottle herself. She jumped in her freshly washed X5 and enjoyed the warm breeze on the ride to Andrea's University City apartment. Andrea had been a client of Selena's for almost five years, and never missed an appointment. Because of her loyalty, she had a head full of healthy, non-chemically treated hair. She was a dark skinned woman with beautiful skin and teeth. There was nothing unique about Andrea's figure, but her personality kept men drawn to her. She was outspoken and adventurous, but knew how to carry herself like a lady.

When Selena got to her door, Andrea greeted her with a huge hug as always, while she finished releasing the last pins in her hair. She let the pin curls bounce and dangle right above her shoulders. She said all she needed to do was throw on her shoes, and they would be on their way.

"No rush girl, take your time. What's that you have on?" Selena asked as Andrea's perfume lingered.

Selena made a face of disapproval as Andrea walked off. She wiped her shoulders off, hoping the fragrance wouldn't cling to her and clash with her Emilio Pucci.

"It's Paris Hilton, don't it smell good?"

"I never really smelled it before. You just have so much on, but it's not bad."

Selena didn't want to hurt Andréa's feelings. She hated Paris Hilton more than the Lolita Lempicka that her sister always wore.

Andrea opted for a pair of Capri jeans, a black fitted crop top, and a pair of black wedge heels. Andrea was the queen of accessories. Anyone who walked through Kouture Kuts selling jewelry knew that if Andrea was in the salon, they had a sale. She wore what had to be the world's largest pair of rhinestone hoop earrings, because they were still visible under her full head of pin curls, a matching bracelet that spiraled from her wrist to her forearm, and a necklace with a rhinestone heart charm that stopped right where her crop top ended, and her belly button began. The pair, against Selena's initial refusal, took a shot of tequila and was on their way.

The ride to Copa's was full of non-stop laughter. Andrea always had the sense of humor that reminded Selena of Tamara. They both always had a quick-witted answer to any question, and knew how to find the humor in any event. As they walked up to the door, Selena felt almost nervous and uneasy. She wasn't really into going out unless it was with Sean or her sister, two people who were no longer a part of her life. The nightlife scene was foreign to her. She felt as if she stood out like a sore thumb, even though that was far from the truth.

They stood in the line for no more than two minutes when a short dark skinned brother yelled out Andrea's name. She turned, recognized the face, and grabbed Selena's hand as they made their way out of the line and up to the front.

"Hey Que," said Andrea as she reached down to hug the man who had to be no taller than 5'4".

"You look great, Drea. When you gon' stop playing with a nigga?" he said as his almost crossed eyes looked at Drea like she was on the Value Menu.

"Que, please, you know I love you like a brother."

Selena had to hold in her chuckle as Andrea said it, because behind the little guy's back she was making faces of total disgust.

"Que, this is my girlfriend, Selena. Selena, this is Que, he and I have been friends since forever."

"Nice to meet you beautiful. Damn Drea, ya'll two together are any man's fantasy, chocolate and vanilla."

Andrea playfully let him know he was corny and proceeded to tell him that they were ready to go inside. He walked the ladies past the red velvet rope and had the woman at the front hand them VIP passes.

It wasn't quite packed, but judging by the line outside, it would be shortly. They walked over to the bar in the VIP section, and Andrea did the honors of ordering them two Jolly Ranchers. She knew Selena was primarily a wine drinker, but wanted her to let go and enjoy herself for the night. T.I.'s hit "Bring em' Out" was blasting, and it made Selena think of her niece, Ari. T.I. was her favorite rapper, and she had the biggest teen crush on him. It made Selena smile. For a minute, she was about to go to the bathroom and call her niece, but remembered that she had tried that last month for Ari's birthday, only to find out her number was changed.

Tamara was a nice person, but one thing Selena knew about her sister, was that when she was upset, or she felt as if someone was trying to "play her" as she would usually say, she was quick to forget about them. Changing a phone number and never talking to someone again was not out of character for her at all. Selena was beginning to realize that she was one of the many that had been removed from Tamara's life.

She was in a zone, thinking of her family, until Andrea tapped her and pointed in the direction of a tall, brown skinned dude who looked to be no older than 24.

"Chile please, he looks closer to Ari's age than mine." Selena turned back towards the bar.

"Girl, who cares? That's Omar Henderson, and he keeps looking over here."

"Who?" questioned Selena, still not turning around to see if she even recognized him.

"From the Miami Heat, the NBA team. There was a game tonight at the Wachovia. This is the after party. That's why it's such a line to get in here. I'm glad I ran into Que's corny lil' ass, so we didn't have to wait in line or pay to get up in here. The lil' fat niggas you grow up with are always good for something."

The two hi-fived and laughed like teenagers. Selena's interest was now sparked as she turned towards the man who had a baby face, but definitely a grown man's physique. He had to be about 6'3", and Selena imagined what his body looked like under his clothes. She knew he was chiseled. He was in the NBA, so he had to be in top physical shape. Her confidence was at a ten, until the club got more crowded, and the flock of young twenty-something year old females swarmed around Omar like bees to honey. She knew she had no chance with someone as young as Omar, with these females around. It was a whole other game with them. Selena wasn't a part of it when she was young, so she knew she couldn't compete at her age.

She changed her focal point from Omar to enjoying time with her only friend, and the closest thing to a family that she had, Andrea. By this time, VIP was overflowing with bottles of Rosé, Patron, and everything else top shelf you could think of. Selena was not much of a drinker, so by midnight, she was at her limit. The DJ had the dance floor packed, and from the sky view in the VIP area, everyone looked like ants. Selena was definitely in a groove, swaying her hips from side to side. She was always a good dancer, and was receiving a lot of attention from the fellas in VIP In no time, they were all watching the toned arms of Selena playfully running her fingers through her hair as she rocked to "Say Aah" by Trey Songz.

When the song changed to the reggae set, Selena decided it was time to have a seat. She was hot, her legs were weary, and she could only imagine how her hair and makeup looked. She looked around and quickly spotted Andrea posted up at the bar, talking to a nice looking brother with dreads. They made quick eye contact as Selena gestured with her hand that she would be sitting in the lounge area off to the side. Andrea winked in approval and quickly turned her attention back to her male companion.

Selena walked through the crowded, yet comfortable

VIP section, eyeing an empty seat in the lounge area. Before she could get there, someone grabbed her hand. She looked to her right, and it was none other than Omar Henderson. She tried to gently pull her hand away, but he grabbed it even tighter. She smiled at him and eventually gave in to his playful tugs for her to come his way.

He pulled her close to him, and bent over to whisper his name and inform her that he'd been watching her dance. Selena told him her name, and couldn't help but sniff his fresh fragrance as he continued to whisper in her ear; after all, she barely reached his chest. He wasn't wearing any cologne, but she could definitely smell that he was freshly showered. He smelled of a deodorant soap, and cocoa butter lotion.

"So how old are you, Omar?" Selena asked. "I'm probably old enough to be your mommy." In the back of her mind, Selena hoped that once he heard her age, he wouldn't be turned off.

"I just turned twenty-five two weeks ago, I'm still celebrating."

He wrapped his arms around Selena's tiny frame and began rocking to the music, leaving Selena no other option but to join in. She felt so comfortable in this complete stranger's arms–so warm and protected. She hadn't felt that way since Sean.

He whispered in Selena's ear that he was about to head back to his hotel. She immediately assumed he thought she was a young groupie that was more than willing to join him there.

She pulled away and snapped, "Oh well, I hope you didn't think I was going with you."

He held her chin up and said, "If you wanted to come,

you would be more than welcomed, but I ain't into assuming anything about anyone."

Selena felt a little embarrassed that she had made that assumption, but quickly felt better when he pulled out his iPhone, asked for her number, and said maybe they could go to breakfast before his afternoon flight. She gave him her number, and he wrapped his arms around her again before he walked off into a group of trampy looking women.

Selena didn't know why, but she felt a little irritated by the group of young girls who swarmed around Omar after they parted. She got over it when Andrea walked up to her and asked if she was ready to go.

Selena just couldn't seem to get Omar off her mind, but she knew she had to. By this time, she knew he was laid up in some hotel room, doing God knows what with one or more of those chicks.

When they arrived at Andrea's, Selena said she was too tired to drive home and asked if she could sleep over. Andrea, of course, had no problem with it. After she undressed and washed her face, she hopped right into the twin-sized bed Andrea had in the guest bedroom of her apartment.

Selena was awakened by the sound of her phone's text notification at 7:00 a.m. She was instantly annoyed because she had a headache from drinking, and had planned to sleep in. It was Sunday, the only day her salon was closed. Her first thought was to ignore it, but she was curious to see who it was. Since she was at Andrea's and hadn't talked to Tamara, she had no idea who else would be contacting her at this hour.

She picked her Blackberry up off the nightstand and

saw a text from an unfamiliar number. *Hey Sexy…U Ready to eat?* She knew immediately that it was Omar, and was now smiling from ear to ear.

She ran past the living room and into Andrea's room without knocking, only to barge in on her cuddle session with the dread headed fella from the club. Andrea sat up straight, while the guy never moved. Selena was so embarrassed. She yelled out that she was sorry and quickly shut the door.

She hurried to gather her things, so that she could leave. She didn't know what Andrea's reaction was going to be. Just as she slid on her pants, the door opened. It was Andrea, laughing hysterically. Selena immediately apologized again and assured her that she was on her way out.

"Girl, please. You do not have to leave because of him. It's ok. Did you have something to tell me or what?"

"I mean yeah, but I'm up here acting like a young girl, all pressed and barging into your room. I'm sorry."

"Oh my God! I told you it was fine. You act like you caught me in the middle of riding that nigga or something. Even then, I wouldn't have cared, you know I'm a freak."

"Drea, you are crazy. I was just coming to tell you that Omar just texted me. He wants to go to breakfast. Should I go?"

"See, you better than me. I would have left ya ass a note on your coffee table and been outta here so fast. You damn right you should go."

"I know, but he's so young, and he doesn't even know my age, and—"

Andrea quickly cut her off. "Leen, it's breakfast. With an NBA star, might I add. Forget all that. Go eat and have fun."

"You're right, let me text him back, thanks Drea. I'll call you with all the details."

She grabbed her purse and headed towards the door.

"You better, and call me later so I can give you mine, or the lack thereof," she mumbled while she rolled her eyes.

"Bye Drea, with your crazy ass."

* * * * *

Selena raced home to change her clothes so she could meet up with Omar in Center City at the Four Seasons Hotel. She had no idea what to wear. She didn't want to look like a slut, or like an old lady, either. She opted for a classic look with a pair of vintage jeans, fitted button-up white polo, and a pair of classic Gucci sneakers with the matching pocketbook.

She washed her hair and let it curl naturally. After all the dancing last night, she didn't have one curl left, and didn't have time to do anything to it. She called him from the lobby to let him know she was there. He told her that he would be right down, so they could go to the hotel restaurant and eat.

He walked off the elevator about five minutes later, and the first thing she noticed was his radiant smile. His teeth were pearly white and straight like no one's teeth she had ever seen. His infectious smile, with his high cheekbones, instantly made Selena smile. He wasn't dressed. He looked as if he had just worked out, with a white t-shirt on, navy blue basketball shorts, fresh white socks pulled all the way up to his knees, and a pair of Nike slide on sandals. He walked over to Selena and greeted her with another one of those warm hugs that felt so right to her.

"Good morning, Ms. Selena," he said with a smile.

The Ms. added to her name made her feel even more like an old lady. She couldn't get past the fact that she was seven years older than him, and he didn't even know yet.

"Good Morning, Mr. Omar."

They held hands while they walked over to the restaurant. The pair sat in silence for a few minutes while they both stared at the menu.

"So what do you do for a living? You a student?"

Selena could not help but laugh when he asked if she was a student. She realized he had no idea of her age, and was flattered at the same time that she could still pass for a student.

"No, I'm not a student. I own a hair salon here in Philly. I have for the past six years."

"So you do hair, huh? Can you cut men? I could use a shape up before I catch my flight this afternoon."

"Yeah, whatever."

"I'm serious though. If you know how, hook me up." he smiled and grabbed Selena's hand. "You are definitely gorgeous. I couldn't stop staring at you last night."

"Really? I didn't think you would notice me, being as though you had about thirty tight dress wearing females draped all over you."

They both burst into laughter as the waitress brought over their water and asked if they were ready to order. Selena ordered strawberry pancakes and vanilla hazelnut coffee, while Omar ordered a Western Omelet and orange juice.

They talked and ate for almost two hours. Omar was young, but he was fun and didn't seem to mind when

Selena finally let him in on her age secret. He even told her that it made her more intriguing that she could be her age and still look better than most of the women he knew that were in their twenties. Selena definitely felt a connection with Omar. She liked his youthful, yet serious demeanor. She was physically attracted to him, and the fact that he was an NBA superstar was the icing on the cake. She wanted him, and she was going to play his way in order to get him.

It was almost one in the afternoon when they finished eating and talking. Selena knew he would need to leave for the airport soon. Selena was confident that he enjoyed her company, but she could only wonder with a handsome, rich man who traveled the world and could have just about any woman he wanted, how she would compare. She thought back to Jamaica, and how she had so easily given herself to Lorenzo who was someone she would probably never see again. She hadn't so much as kissed Omar, someone she really felt a connection with.

Omar stood up from the table and reached for her hand. He playfully pulled her close to him, and they walked through the hotel, looking like a couple who had been together for years. Once at the front door of the hotel, Omar turned Selena towards him and bent down to kiss her lips. Selena closed her eyes and waited. The kiss was sweet and gentle, and Selena held him tightly around his waist. He promised to call once his flight landed in Miami, and she promised to visit him soon.

The ride home was silent for Selena. She could barely stop smiling as she drove and thought of the exciting conversation she had just had with Omar Henderson. She had to admit to herself that prior to last night she barely knew who he was. She wasn't a sports fan. She couldn't wait to get home and Google him. She wanted to know everything about him.

Before she arrived at her house, her phone rang. It was none other than Andrea. She reminded Selena of Tamara in so many ways; her timing was perfect. If Selena didn't know any better, she would have thought that Andrea was spying on her.

"Hey Drea."

"Don't hey Drea, me. DETAILS!" she hollered.

Selena played it cool.

"Details about what? We had a really nice breakfast. He said he would call when he got to Miami."

"Bitch, don't play with me. So you ain't give that nigga none?" she asked in her most ghetto voice.

"Noooo, we had really great conversation. I didn't feel the need to, besides, I ain't one of these lil' hot in the panty ass young girls trying to get somebody to claim me."

"That's exactly why you should have put that shit on his young ass, 'cause these young girls are vicious out here. You leaving the gate open for they asses." She let out a huge sigh of disappointment.

Selena, in her heart, knew she had handled it in the most appropriate way for her. But after Drea brought some things to her attention, it did make her wonder. However, she would never let Drea or anyone else know that she was questioning her decision.

"Well, I'm sorry that me not giving up my pussy, has you so upset," she said, and burst into laughter. "Besides, I'm going to Miami to see him next week, and you better believe I'm going to handle my business," Selena lied.

They hadn't set up a definite date for her to come, but

she knew she wanted it to be as soon as possible. She wasn't letting Omar get away that easy.

"Now that's my girl, I knew you had something up your sleeve."

The two chatted like high school girls until Selena pulled into her driveway. She finished her conversation with Drea before telling her that she would call her later after she got settled and showered.

Selena was happy to be at home. She poured herself a glass of Merlot, headed up the stairs, and began to run a bath filled with lavender and vanilla bubble bath. She slipped out of her clothing and walked slowly to her bathroom with the glass of wine in her hand. She loved hip-hop and R&B music, but when she wanted to relax, she loved listening to jazz and soul music from as early as the 50's.

She turned up her surround sound stereo system as she lay in the warm water, sipping wine and listening to Etta James sing about her "Sunday Kind of Love." She enjoyed the symphonic sounds as she lay back and thought of her life; the good, the bad, and the portions she had no idea about. Although she had a lot to question, she was still grateful, and appreciative to be who she was and to have what she had. She vowed to never look back, never regret, and to live life like there was no tomorrow.

* * * * *

It had been almost three months since Selena had initially met Omar, and they were still in contact. The first month she had only seen him two times because of work, and his team making it to the playoffs. But by July, she was spending at least two weekends a month in Miami, going down on Saturday nights and coming home on Monday nights. Just enough time to get home, get some rest, and be ready for work on Tuesday morning. He was still every bit of a gentleman, and even bought Selena nice gifts almost every time they saw each other.

Selena was having fun getting to know Omar and being showered with gifts. Sean had taken good care of Selena, but this was different. It was beyond basic needs and an occasional splurge on a pair of expensive shoes. He paid for her airfare each time she traveled, designer bags were given on a regular basis, jewelry gifts were frequent, and he was even hinting around about buying her a car for her upcoming birthday.

Selena enjoyed the lifestyle, and she wanted Omar all to herself. She could look past his constant travel, groupies, and even the fact that he didn't really know how to satisfy her sexually. She found herself on a few different occasions working extra hard to arouse him. She knew he saw other women, and had no problem working harder to keep him interested. He lacked passion, and sometimes seemed afraid to explore her body like she needed him to. But he was younger than her, and she was willing to teach him, because of the perks of being with him.

Selena lay on the beach in her bright orange swimsuit with her red tinted hair pulled up in a neat bun, and a pair of white Gucci sunglasses given to her by Omar. He was working out with some friends, so Selena decided to take in some sun and regroup before her flight back to Philly tomorrow. She was tired of traveling back and forth, but she and Omar hadn't become exclusive yet, and she didn't think he was ready to let go of the other females he was dealing with.

Her phone rang and she answered it without looking. "Hello."

"Hey girl," the voice on the other end replied.

It was Andrea, and for the past month or so, she had become quite annoying to Selena.

"Hey," she answered blandly.

"I sent you a message on Facebook yesterday. I thought you would have called me by now. Y'all must be living it up," she said in a sarcastic voice.

"Now you know damn well I don't be on that shit like that. I use it primarily for the salon to promote specials, but what's up?" she asked in an almost annoyed voice.

"I was tryna see if you were going to the event that Omar is hosting tonight down there. I hear its red carpet and everything. It's some type of party to benefit breast cancer, and everyone from Kim Kardashian to Chris Brown are supposed to be there. Fat ass from Copa is flying down on some buddy passes later, and I would come if you are gonna be there. We haven't partied together in a minute."

Selena was instantly irritated that Omar hadn't so much as said one word about this event he was hosting. Now that Andrea mentioned it, he did ask her more than once today if her flight was tonight or tomorrow, and her flights were always on Mondays.

"I'm not going. He is only stopping by for about an hour because he got paid for it already, and then we're chillin'. You know my flight is in the morning."

Selena lied because she didn't want Andrea to know that Omar hadn't told her about it. Andrea quickly ended the conversation after she found out that Selena wasn't attending. That was another reason Selena had started to distance herself from her. It seemed like she only wanted to be around if she thought there was a chance she could meet a celebrity.

Selena wrapped her towel around her waist and headed back to Omar's condo. He had better have a good excuse as to why he hadn't mentioned the event to her. She had just enough time to shower before Omar returned from working out.

* * * * *

He looked exhausted, and threw himself on his black leather sofa when he walked in the door.

Selena came out of the bedroom naked, her hair still wet and curly hanging on her shoulders. Her dainty footsteps echoed on the tiled floors of the condo. Omar looked up and began to smile as her saw her walking towards him slowly, her belly button ring dangling and her fragrance lingering. He stood up and reached out for her, and she playfully pulled back. He reached out further, and she took off running. Omar followed quickly behind and caught her not even ten seconds later. They stood in the foyer and began to kiss. He was excited, and he started to come out of his tank top.

Selena quickly halted the kissing fest and asked him why he hadn't told her about the event. He looked confused, and wondered why she chose now of all times, to ask a question. He wanted her, and didn't feel like talking. Selena was serious, though. She started to realize that she had never been anywhere of importance with Omar in the months they had been seeing each other.

Yes, they would go to dinner, or to a movie, but for the most part, they spent 85% of their time in Omar's condo. Even when he bought her things, he would always go out and bring the items back. She wasn't even invited to his teammate's birthday bash last month, and when she saw the pictures on the internet, everyone else had a date.

"So what's up, Omar? How come you didn't ask me to go to the event tonight?"

"You serious, you're mad? I just thought you didn't wanna go. You always talk about being older and not feeling like partying, so why even bother?"

"I mean, yeah, if I'm just in Philly and it's just going out to go out, but if I'm in Miami *with you*, and you're hosting an event or its one of your friends' party, that's different. An invite is always nice, whether I accept or not. So what, it's just leave the old chick in the crib and go party with the young girls?"

"Come on now with that. It ain't even like that."

He was now annoyed and walked away from Selena. He went in the kitchen and grabbed a bottled water from the refrigerator. Selena had slipped into a nightgown, plopped down on the couch, and sat in silence.

After about five minutes, Selena turned and yelled, "So you're not gonna say anything? We're just gonna sit in silence like two kids in trouble?"

Omar ignored her, went into his bedroom, and closed the door. Selena followed behind him and pushed the door open.

"I'm confused. What's up? I ask you a question, and instead of us talking about it, you give me the silent treatment and walk off like a lil' kid?"

"Listen, I'm not your age, but I'm not a kid. I don't

get questioned by anyone. I didn't ask you to go because I didn't want you to go. It's as simple as that. We're not married. I owe you no explanations, just like you owe me none. We spend time together because we want to, not because we *have* to."

Selena stood stunned by the man who was always so kind and playful. He was actually trying to put her in some kind of place. Although she felt hurt, she knew Omar was right. They had no commitment, and neither one of them had to explain anything to the other.

After a brief, awkward silence, she gently whispered, "You are absolutely right, and it is also a free country, right?

She walked over to her suitcase and pulled out a slinky black dress and her sexy black pumps.

"What are you doing?"

"I'm getting dressed to go to the event. I don't come to Miami just to sit in the house and eat. I can catch a cab." She scurried around the condo, gathering her accessories and putting on her makeup.

Omar burst into laughter. He stood against the bedroom door while she prepared to go out while talking to herself. "What's funny?" Selena snapped.

"You are. If you wanted to go, all you had to do was ask. I don't have a problem taking you anywhere. You always want to act like a little homebody. Let me throw my clothes on, and we can be on our way."

Selena was excited. She didn't think it would be this easy. This would be their first time out in public since the night they met. She couldn't wait to see what his interaction would be amongst others. As she put the finishing touches on her makeup, her phone started to ring. She looked at her caller ID, and it was Tamara. She wanted to answer, because she had already had to cancel their lunch date, but she needed to get ready. Omar would be ready any minute. A few minutes later, a new voicemail notification popped up. Just as Selena was picking up her phone to return her sister's call, Omar announced that he was ready. She quickly placed her phone in her purse and wrapped her arm around Omar's.

The club was packed. There was no VIP, and the groupies, female and male were all over the place. Tight dresses, pounds of makeup, and stares filled the room. Omar mingled. He introduced Selena to a few people, which made her smile, but there were a few looks and stares that annoyed her. One male in particular stared at Omar until he got his attention. He gave him a look that was as sharp as a knife. Omar frowned and looked away.

He grabbed Selena by her waist, and pulled her in closer to speak into her ear. "Man, niggas be on some other shit. I can feel the hate from across the room."

Selena giggled and reached up to wrap her arms around Omar's neck. She was making it known that he was her man. She secretly prayed that paparazzi were snapping pictures of her and Omar. They remained at that party until almost 1:00 a.m., then decided they had enough and were ready to go.

She had enjoyed her visit with Omar, but knew her reality was that she wasn't happy. On the flight home, Selena thought about everything from Sean, to Tamara, to Omar. She wanted to live happily ever after, but the tale of her life was far from anything magical. She knew nothing about her history, her life was a lie, and she had no one to love her completely.

She knew that she had to call Tamara when she got back home. Not only had she left a voicemail, but she had also texted her. The salon was the only thing left in her life that was truly her own, and even that wasn't the same. She no longer had the passion to style hair, her clientele had changed, and it wasn't fun to her anymore. She wanted out. If her life was going to get better, she had to make it that way. Everything from her past had to go, salon included.

* * * * *

She arrived home at about 4:00 p.m., and was exhausted. She didn't even unpack her bag before she turned her shower on and stood in the steamy stall. The scent of her Coconut Vanilla body wash calmed her nerves and eased her mind. There was something about fragrance that soothed Selena. She could have had a horrible day, but after a hot shower and a spray or two of a lovely fragrance, she was right back where she needed to be.

Even though she was extremely tired, she still couldn't fall asleep once she lay in the bed. She decided to pull out her laptop and surf the internet. She ended up on Facebook. She hardly ever used the social networking site, but every once in a while, she would log in just to see what was going on. Her page was listed under the salon name, and she had nothing personal on her page. All the photos were of clients, and the only posts made by Selena were specials at the salon. Once she was logged in, she had thirty-two friend requests, twelve inbox messages, and twenty-four other requests.

She clicked on the friend requests first, and was amazed

at all the people she remembered from high school and college who had requested her. She accepted them all. Then she went over to her inbox. They were all event invitations except two; one from Andrea Gray, the message she said she had sent on Saturday about her coming to Miami, and one message from someone named ARI MS HOLLISTER. She didn't know who it was at first. She looked closer at the profile picture, and realized it was Arielle, her niece. She had only seen her once since she and Tamara had spoken.

Selena quickly clicked on the message and waited for what seemed like forever until the message displayed. It had been sent a few hours ago, and she didn't want her niece to think she was ignoring her. She sat quietly and read the message from her baby girl.

Hey Aunt Leeni, it's me, Ari. I miss u so much. I tried to call you but I kept getting voicemail. If I have never needed u b4, I need u now. I am so scared of what will happen if my mom finds out I am pregnant. She is already stressed enough about money and losing one of her biggest clients, and I'm just making it worse. I am not ready to be a mom. I need help. School starts in a couple of weeks and I don't want to go to school pregnant. I am so embarrassed. Please call me or write back....something Aunt Leeni.

Selena cried as she wrote back to her niece. She asked her if she was she near her mom, and if she could talk. Arielle responded quickly and said that her mom was right there. She had called before she got home, but now Facebook was the best option to communicate. She knew that she must be scared, and she also knew that her sister would definitely have a cow if she knew that Arielle was having sex, let alone pregnant. She let her know that she missed her too, and told her that she would do anything to help her, and to meet her at the salon the next day.

Selena knew that Arielle was referring to helping her get an abortion. If Tamara ever found out that she went behind her back and took her daughter to get an abortion, she would be devastated, and it would most likely ruin any chance of them repairing their relationship. She knew it was wrong to go behind her back, but Tamara had lied to her for years about her life, and Arielle was not ready to be a mother. She was willing to risk her and Tamara's sisterhood, for Arielle's chance to live a normal life and fulfill her dreams.

CHAPTER 6

Selena knew that her last client would be out of there by 4 p.m., and that was around the time Arielle would arrive. She couldn't wait to see her niece walk through her salon doors. Her last client walked out at 4:03 and Arielle, dressed in a pair of jean Capris, a fitted navy blue and white Abercrombie tee shirt, and a pair of navy blue Polo canvas sneakers entered the place at 4:19 p.m. Her hair was longer than it had ever been, hanging just about four inches inch away from her shoulders. It was bone straight with blonde highlights. Selena couldn't believe that Tamara actually let her color her hair, and she wondered who had done the job. Selena had been the only person to touch Arielle's hair since she was a baby.

Arielle rushed to Selena, who she was taller than, and threw her arms around her. They held each other tightly for almost two minutes as silent tears rolled down each of their faces. Selena pulled back from the hug when she heard Ari sniffling from crying. She took her thumbs and gently wiped her eyes.

"Don't cry baby girl. I'm here for you, and I'm never going anywhere, EVER."

They walked over to the waiting area of the salon, and sat like two teenage girls and talked. Selena didn't want to rush into the conversation about the pregnancy, so she let Ari lead, for the most part. She talked about meeting her Grandpa for the first and only time, which initially puzzled Selena. She thought for sure that when Carl was released from prison, that he'd stay with Tamara and Arielle, and become reacquainted.

The truth was that when Carl was released, he was dying of brain cancer. He was very sick, she explained, he only weighed one hundred pounds. Tamara had put him right into a hospice where he lived only thirty-two days. She told her aunt that her mother didn't seem the same since he had died. Her life had revolved around work until the recent loss of her biggest client, a huge hotel chain that she had since the inception of her business. She barely paid attention to anything else. Everything was based around trying to get her business back where it used to be. This was how Ari said she began hanging more with her friends. Her father had moved three months ago to Atlanta for his job, and she wasn't going to see him again until Christmas.

"Did you tell the boy?" Selena couldn't wait any longer. She wanted to know everything.

"Yes, he was upset. He said that I had to do something about it, and quick."

Although Selena knew that having a baby was not what Arielle needed to be doing at this time, she was irritated that the person who helped her get into that condition was so nonchalant about it. Instead of making matters worse, she decided not to ask any more questions about the little asshole who had impregnated her niece. She would solely focus on her.

"So when was your last period, Ari?"

She held her head down. "I don't know the exact date, but it was in June. It only lasted like two days, and it never came in July."

Tears started to run down Arielle's face as well as Selena's. She thought back to the moment she was born, and couldn't believe that she was in this situation; sixteen and pregnant.

"Well, first things first. We have to go find out exactly how far along you are, so we can schedule the appointment. I will make you an appointment in the morning. You know this has to stay between you and me, right?"

"Yes, Aunt Leeni."

"And Ari, know this," she continued in a stern yet concerned voice, "this is the last time I am going to do this for you. We will look into birth control options, and you will focus on your school work and going on to college. There is plenty of time for all of that other stuff you are trying to rush into, do you understand?"

Arielle nodded in agreement.

It was getting late, and Selena knew that Tamara would be arriving home from work within the hour, so she and Arielle headed towards Glad Wynne. She made a stop at Friendly's first to get her princess a banana split, before dropping her off on the corner of the subdivision. She reminded Ari to keep quiet about their meeting, and that she would call her tomorrow with her appointment date.

She sat on the corner and watched Arielle walk off into the sunset. She was no longer her little princess. She was changing. Her silhouette in the setting sun confirmed Selena's thoughts.

* * * * *

Selena wasted no time scheduling an appointment at her Center City gynecologist's office for Arielle. They were able to schedule her for the following Monday at 10:00 a.m. She texted Arielle and informed her of the appointment day and time. Selena was bored. Since Sean died, she didn't have the passion to style hair that she used to, and business wasn't the same. A majority of her clientele, she had to admit, were Sean's family and friends. Marissa, his sister had only been to the salon twice since he passed, and she and some of her friends were regulars in Selena's book. If Selena hadn't been the type to save money and handle her finances properly, she could easily be suffering from hard times.

As she sat in the shop reading *Cosmopolitan* and smelling the samples of fragrances in the magazine, she decided that she wanted out of the salon. She didn't know what exactly she was going to do afterward. For sure, after she handled Arielle's situation, she would be looking for a real estate agent to help her sell the salon.

* * * * *

It was Monday morning, and Selena couldn't wait to see her Arielle again. She wished it wasn't under these circumstances, and she'd even hoped for life how it used to be when she, Arielle, and Tamara did everything together. Since she had met with Arielle last week, she had thought so many times to call her sister and tell her what was going on, so they could handle it like a family. However, she knew there were too many other issues at hand with her and Tamara that needed to be dealt with separately, and Ari would be forever hurt if Selena told her mother what she had confided in her.

Tamara left for work at 8:30 every morning, so they arranged for her to pick up Arielle at 9:00 a.m., which would give them enough time to grab something to eat before her appointment. Arielle stepped out of the door with her hair pulled back in a tight, neat ponytail and a hot pink and green sundress with matching pink sandals. She looked like a little girl again– the little girl that Selena wanted her to be so badly. She plopped in the car and immediately asked Selena to turn the air up as she unscrewed the cap of her Deer Park water. It was smoldering hot outside during this end of August heat wave.

Selena smiled as she smelled the fresh scent of Dolce & Gabbana's Light Blue, lingering on Arielle.

"Light Blue, huh Ari? Classic, I taught you well. Is your mother still wearing that stinkin' ass Lolita Lempicka?"

"Yesssssss, oh my God Aunt Leeni. She swears it smells so good."

They burst into laughter and talked and laughed the whole ride downtown. Arielle wasn't hungry. She said that her mother had cooked before she went to work, so Selena just grabbed an iced coffee from Dunkin Donuts before she parked her X5 in the lot directly across from her doctor's office on 16th Street.

Arielle looked nervous as they walked into the office, which was pretty empty for it to be early in the morning. There was one visibly pregnant woman sitting and reading a magazine, a younger girl who looked like she was a college student, and an older woman who appeared to be in her fifties. Arielle sat down closest to the sign in sheet as Selena went over and signed her in.

Selena pulled out her credit card to pay the $50.00 office visit fee, because even though Arielle had insurance, it was through Tamara, and she didn't want her to know anything about this. It was only about twenty minutes before the nurse called Arielle to the back.

Initially, Selena stayed seated until she looked up and noticed Ari waiting by the door as if she wanted Selena to accompany her. They went in the back room where the nurse came in and asked a few questions, before giving Arielle a container to put her urine specimen in. Once she came back from the bathroom, she was instructed to get undressed and to put on the hospital gown.

It was cold in the office, and Arielle looked nervous. Selena stood up and wrapped her arms around her, letting her know that she would be ok. Dr. Spencer knocked and waited a few seconds before she walked in. She greeted Selena and complimented her fragrance as she always did whenever Selena was in the office. She had been Selena's GYN since she was eighteen years old, and she had aged beautifully. She had to be well into her fifties with the prettiest gray hair that she wore naturally curly and short, and smooth caramel brown skin. She was always well dressed, and had the classiest shoe collection that Selena had ever seen.

Today, she opted for a pair of Prada peep toe pumps. She began by asking Arielle questions pertaining to her menstrual cycle and sexual history. She seemed nervous at first, but Dr. Spencer assured her that everything was just fine and that she was there to help her.

Once the urine tests came back, Dr. Spencer confirmed

the pregnancy and did an exam of her abdomen. She estimated Arielle to be about 10 weeks pregnant. An ultrasound technician came into the room with a portable ultrasound machine and performed the ultrasound that put Arielle's fetus at 10 weeks and 2 days. Selena spoke with Dr. Spencer in Arielle's presence and explained that she wanted to terminate the pregnancy.

Dr. Spencer spoke to Arielle, gave her a lot of information on the procedure, and made sure that the decision to abort was clearly Arielle's and no one else's. Before leaving the office, they scheduled Arielle's procedure in the same building, but a different office. Dr. Spencer referred patients who did not want to carry their pregnancy full-term to Dr. Matar. It was set for Saturday. Arielle would be back to herself again soon, able to start her junior year of high school without the worries of motherhood, relationships, or heartache. She was starting over.

* * * * *

Arielle usually went to modeling class on Saturday mornings, which worked out perfectly. Once Tamara dropped her off at the corner of 15th and Spruce to attend a class at John Robert Powers, she would walk over two blocks to meet her aunt at the doctor's office.

Tamara let the window down after Arielle got out of the car, to make sure she had her money and cell phone charger since she would be traveling to Kierra's after "class." Tamara was going to New York for a meeting with a potential client, so Arielle would be sleeping over at Kierra's. Although she never minded hanging with her BFF Kierra, this was exactly the change that Arielle was talking about. Tamara almost never did anything with her anymore. She assured her mother that she had everything, and they both yelled "I love you" at the same time, as Tamara pulled off when the light changed to green.

Arielle called Selena and let her know that she was on her way over as she began walking down Walnut Street. The walk seemed to take forever. She couldn't believe she was even pregnant, let alone about to have an abortion. Selena sat patiently in the waiting room, carrying a huge black Michael Kors bag.

It was packed in the doctor's office. Older women, younger women, black, white, Spanish, Asian, it was truly a diverse group. She looked around the room until she noticed her aunt sitting towards the back, with her signature huge sunglasses on. She smiled and made her way to her. There wasn't a seat directly next to her, so she had to sit in a seat in front of her.

There was paperwork to fill out, and blood work to be done, then Selena would pay for the procedure, followed by waiting, waiting and more waiting before they finally called Arielle to the back. She hugged her aunt and walked through the heavy wooden door.

Once she was in the back, she walked slowly down the hallway. On the left was a room where some females were sitting with hospital gowns on, looking like they were tired. She looked on the door, and the sign read RECOVERY. The nurse led her back to a changing room where she was to undress and leave all of her belongings and put the gown on. She was nervous, yet at ease. The nurse was friendly. It smelled clean in the office, and the rooms were sparkling clean.

She made her way to room #5, as the nurse instructed,

and waited about ten minutes for the dark Indian man with the heavy accent named Dr. Matar to appear. The nurse walked in at the same time, and they both explained that they would be giving her medication via injection to make her sleepy so that she wouldn't feel or remember the procedure. They explained that they would be attaching a small machine that functioned similar to a vacuum cleaner to her uterus, and that once they turned it on, it would gently remove the fetus.

She knew that she would then be transferred to the room she had just walked past, to fully regain her senses and prepare to be discharged from the facility. Within minutes of receiving the medication, she began to feel tired. When she awakened, she was being wheeled into the recovery room.

She felt nauseous. When the nurse came in, she gave her a small container to use in case she needed to throw up. She felt a little crampy and was given two pills. One, the nurse said was for pain; the other was to reduce the risk of infection. She rested in recovery for about forty-five minutes before they gave her discharge instructions and two containers with the pills in them. She was advised to rest over the next few days, not to have sex, take soak baths, and to take her medication until it was gone. She would have to come back for a follow up appointment in the next couple of weeks.

Arielle got dressed and made her way out to the waiting room where her aunt waited for her. There were only a few people left in the waiting room, and Arielle was ready to go. They waited until they got out in the hallway of the office to hug. Arielle fought back tears as she rested her head on her aunt's shoulder, inhaling the scent of her beautiful fragrance. She was not only crying about the procedure, but because she was hiding something from her mother. She wished things could be like they used to be. She somehow thought that if Aunt Leeni and her mother hadn't stopped talking, she would have never gotten pregnant. They held hands and walked silently until they reached the car.

"I wish you could come home with me, Arielle, so I could take care of you. You have to make sure you are resting and taking those medications."

"I will, Aunt Leeni. I just can't wait to get to Kierra's house so I can sleep. I'm tired," she yawned.

"Yes, baby girl, you need your rest. Do you want to stop at the store to get anything in particular to eat?"

She declined, and reminded her aunt that Kierra's mom, whom she called Auntie Marie always had something tasty cooking, and their house always had plenty of food. They sat in the car in front of Kierra's house for almost twenty minutes before Arielle got out of the truck. They hugged once again, and Arielle was on her way.

Selena waited way past Arielle actually getting in the house. She sat an additional five minutes, reflecting on what she had just done. She realized it was the best decision for Arielle at the time, but she knew that even after the lie Tamara had told her, what she had done, was wrong.

Arielle hadn't even told Kierra, her best friend, because of the embarrassment. She simply told her that she was crampy because her period had come on while she was at modeling class. The girls headed up to Kierra's bedroom, stopping at Marie's room to say hello and give her a hug first.

"Hey sweetie pie!" she exclaimed as she sat on the edge of her bed watching DVR'd episodes of Real Housewives of New Jersey. Marie was a pretty woman with a round face, long, thick hair, and a light complexion adorned with freckles all over her face. She was short and round. Kierra was short as well, and always pouted that once she hit thirty she would lose what was labeled "thick" and turn into her mother.

She reached over and hugged Marie.

"You feel warm sweetie, you ok?"

"Yes, Auntie I'm fine. I've been crampy with a headache all day. My period came on today," she lied.

"Well yup, that will do it. I made some lasagna last night, and there's plenty left. Get you something to eat and drink, and go lie down. If ya'll don't sit up all night giggling, maybe you can get some rest."

They all laughed as the girls walked out of her room.

Arielle pulled out her phone and texted her mother: *@ Kierra's now mom... I love you.* She then texted Brian, the young man who had impregnated her to let him know: *I did it.*

Tamara was the first to respond. *Ok sweetie. I will be there around noon tomorrow for u. What about a mani and a pedi? I love u too.*

Arielle was excited. She and Tamara hadn't been spending much time together lately. This was exactly what they needed. She was feeling great about her decision not to keep the baby. *I can't wait* she responded to Tamara's text.

Brian texted back almost ten minutes later, and the only thing he said was, *Good.*

Arielle felt hurt by his lack of interest, but still decided to text him again. *WYD*

He responded. *Nuttin'*.

She placed her phone on Kierra's nightstand and looked over to notice Kierra giggling and texting away.

She told her that she was going downstairs to get something to eat, and that she would be right back. She went into the bathroom and felt like she needed to throw up. She was hot and felt dizzy. It took her almost ten minutes to change her pad as she felt like she was going to pass out. She was bleeding heavier than her period, and the pain medication hadn't kicked in yet.

She got back to Kierra's room and picked up her iPhone to see if she had any missed calls or texts, there were none. She laid across Kierra's bed, and pretended to listen to her talk about some type of argument she was having via Facebook until she drifted off to sleep.

* * * * *

Selena dreaded answering Andrea's call, but knew she was calling to check on Arielle. Selena had slipped, and told her, when Andrea wondered why she had to reschedule her normal Saturday appointment at the salon. Although Andrea had ways about her that annoyed the hell out of Selena, she always listened, was a loyal customer, and someone to talk to, especially since she couldn't talk to Tamara.

They chatted briefly about Arielle and the procedure until Andrea casually brought up Omar, as she usually did. This was when Selena usually ended the conversation. She couldn't understand why Andrea always wanted to talk about Omar, and was always asking if they were truly a couple, and how long she thought they would deal with each other. Selena had strong feelings for Omar, and she didn't know why. She was always into committed relationships, never just flings. What she and Omar had was simply that, and she knew it. Her plans to sell the salon and relocate to Miami would increase her chances of creating a relationship with Omar. She sipped on a glass of White Zinfandel, and pondered the future until she fell off to sleep.

* * * * *

Arielle opened her eyes and felt blinded by the sunlight that peeked in Kierra's window. She looked over to the other twin bed where Kierra was still asleep, and felt bad that she hadn't shared her secret with her best friend since the age of eight. She decided that after she showered and got dressed, she'd tell her. She needed someone to talk to. She sat up straight in the bed and still had the same headache from last night, the same nausea, and she still felt warm.

She flipped the sheet back that she had slept under, so she could get out of bed to grab her medication from of her bag. She looked down at the bed and realized she had bled all over Kierra's bed. She grabbed her head in embarrassment and stood up quickly to try to get to the bathroom. She was a bloody mess, and when she went to take a step over to the dresser to grab her pocketbook, she felt weak. Her legs got wobbly, and she passed out. She hit her head on the dresser on the way down.

Kierra heard the thump and jumped up. "Ari!" she screamed. "What is wrong!?"

She started to cry, and ran to get her mother, who was already running down the hall to see what all the noise was.

Maria kneeled down next to Arielle and gently tapped her face, trying to get her to respond. "Ari!" she yelled.

"What were you two doing in here, Kierra?" she demanded.

"We were sleep, Mom. I woke up when I heard a bang, and when I looked up, she was on the floor. I don't know, Mommy, I'm scared."

"It's ok, baby. First call 911, and then give Tamara a call."

Arielle was breathing and trying to open her eyes. Marie continued to hold her, confused as to what caused her to pass out in the first place. Her night shorts were soaked in blood, and when Kierra came back in the room, she noticed that the bed was a mess, as well. Maria had come to the conclusion that she was bleeding heavily due to her period and that she had gotten dizzy and passed out.

Within minutes, the ambulance was pulling into the driveway at 675 Hamilton Ave. Tamara arrived only 5 minutes after they did.

Arielle was conscious and speaking by the time Tamara arrived. She had told the EMTs and Marie the reason behind the bleeding, but when her mother asked her, she didn't respond. Tamara wiped tears from under Arielle's eyes and kissed the bruise that had appeared on her head from the dresser she hit on the way to the floor. She stood in the driveway and waited for them to lift Arielle into the ambulance so that she could follow them. Marie walked over to Tamara and gave her a hug. She knew she had to tell Tamara the information that Arielle had given her.

"T, Arielle is bleeding heavy and feeling sick because yesterday she had an abortion," she said, and waited nervously for a response.

"WHAT, Maria are you crazy? Arielle went to modeling yesterday and then here—" she stopped in mid-sentence and became angry. "You took my daughter to have an abortion behind my back?"

"First off, calm down, and hell no, I would never do anything like that to you or Arielle. I have too much love for the both of you—"

Tamara cut her off to give her a hug and apologize.

"It's ok, but I have to tell you. Your sister took her."

"This is some typical Selena shit! I can't believe she took my daughter to get an abortion behind my back and didn't even have the decency to let an adult know so that someone could look after her properly. This is some bullshit!" she screamed.

"I know T, and she was wrong. Right now, let's focus on Ari, and making sure she is ok. I will drive, and we can follow the ambulance. You don't need to be driving right now."

Tamara didn't respond. She just followed behind Marie and hopped into her Gold SUV.

The wait at the hospital seemed like forever. Tamara, who rarely showed her emotional side, could barely control herself as she cried. The tears were not only because her daughter was lying in a hospital bed, but because of the mere fact that she felt like she couldn't talk to her about it. Had Tamara been that distant to not even realize that her own daughter was pregnant? And how could Selena go behind her back? Her thoughts were racing. She wanted to see Arielle, and her patience was running thin.

It was another hour before the doctor came out to speak with Tamara. She was tired, upset, and nervous all at once, but when she saw the doctor heading her way, she found the energy to pull it all together and stand up straight to hear about her baby girl.

"Hi Ms. Nichols, I'm Dr. Williams. Your daughter is resting right now and doing much better. She experienced an incomplete abortion."

She saw the puzzled look on Tamara's face and began to explain in detail. "Basically, an incomplete abortion happens to women who are over 8 weeks pregnant and in Arielle's case, she was a little over 10 weeks. Sometimes the suction and curette do not remove the entire pregnancy from the uterus, which prevents it from starting the process of returning to its natural form. That is why she was bleeding so heavy, feeling dizzy, and beginning to develop a fever. Actually it sounds odd, but her passing out was probably the best thing that could have happened.

"Because she was keeping it a secret, had she not fainted, she probably would have remained in pain and excessive bleeding. That could've led to a serious infection that ultimately could've have cost her life. We performed a D&C on her to totally remove the pregnancy, and are giving her antibiotics through an IV to ward off any potential infection. You can see her if you like."

"Thank you so much, doctor."

She was anxious to see her, but knew that Maria and Kierra wanted to see her, as well. Since she knew she was all right, she allowed them to go in first so that once they were done, she could sit and speak with her daughter alone. Besides, while they were visiting, she could call Selena and let her know the chaos she had caused. She pulled out her Blackberry, only to realize it was completely dead. She asked one of the nurses if there was a phone she could use, and she pointed her in the direction.

Tamara actually felt nervous while calling Selena. She hadn't heard her voice in a while, and missed her sister. This wasn't going to be a sweet reunion. Selena had violated, and she needed her to know that. She answered the phone on the third ring in a very bland tone.

"Yes."

"Yeah, Selena, it's Tamara. What type of shit are you into? First, you find out my sixteen year old daughter is pregnant, and don't tell me. You take her to get an abortion, still fuck Tamara who happens to be her mother. Then you drop her off, not even at home, but at someone else's home. She becomes their responsibility, yet you don't even let them in on the secret. And now, my daughter is laying up in fuckin' Bryn Mawr hospital because of it. Did you think you were helping Arielle out by trying to hide something from me? Huh? Because you didn't."

Selena couldn't believe it. Why didn't she just tell Tamara? She knew she was wrong, but she always had a hard time admitting it. She tried to shift the conversation back to Arielle's well-being.

"Oh my God, is she ok? I'm on my way, T, I—"

She was interrupted by an angry Tamara.

"Don't fuckin' T me, and don't dare bring ya ass down here. I'm her mother, and I said you can't see her, so don't waste your time. I know you probably thought you were helping Arielle, but all you did was teach her how to be sneaky and land her in the hospital. To ease your mind, she will be fine, and *we* will be great without you. *stay the fuck away from me and my daughter!*"

She slammed the phone down, and looked around at some people who were looking at her strangely, due to her tirade. She returned their stares and walked with pride back to Arielle's room.

Kierra and Marie were giving hugs to Ari as Tamara walked in. Her face looked as if she did not want them to leave now that her mother had walked in the room. She knew her mother was upset, and she had every right to be. It was time to face the music. Tamara, Maria, and Kierra group hugged and said their goodbyes. Tamara then walked over to Arielle and kissed her on the forehead and sat in the seat right next to the bed.

"Arielle, I am so grateful that you are okay," she spoke tearfully and full of emotion. "But I am so upset that you felt like you couldn't talk to me about it. Why would you keep this from Mommy? We talk about everything. You're my best friend." She reached out and grabbed her hand, held it tightly, and pulled it to her lips to kiss.

Arielle sat up in the hospital bed, eyes flooded with tears.

"Talk to me Ari, what is it?"

She let the quarter sized tears slowly roll down her face and drop like raindrops onto her hospital gown before she started to speak.

"We just haven't been the same, Mommy. Ever since you and Aunt Leeni haven't spoken, and your dad died, all you cared about was work. I mean, I know you love me, but it just seems so different. I made a mistake, and I'm sorry Mommy. Please don't be mad at Aunt Leeni, I begged her not to tell you."

Her words were sincere and heartfelt, and as much as Tamara didn't want to be mad at Selena, she already was, and the damage was done. She stood up and wrapped her arms around her daughter. She stroked her hair and told her that everything would be all right.

CHAPTER 7

It was Monday afternoon, when Selena woke up. After the phone call she received from her sister, she had drank an entire bottle of Zinfandel and fell asleep. She sat on her king sized bed, looking at the mess that was considered her room. There were clothes everywhere, unpacked luggage bags from her back and forth excursions to Miami, and dust all over her black oak dresser, but what stood out the most was her perfume collection. It was usually in order by color, height, and of course, frequency of use. Right now, however, it was in complete disarray, similar to her life.

She usually felt strong, independent, in control, and organized like a bottle of Gucci Rush. These days she's been more weak, watered down, and vulnerable; reminiscent of Glo by J.Lo. Selena had to make a change, in her love life, career, friendships, and most importantly, herself. She was starting her evolution today. Everything was about Selena, no looking back. She knew her sister well enough to know that she meant what she said. As much as she loved Tamara and Arielle, and as hurt as she was that her deceit landed her niece in the hospital, she knew she had to move on.

The first order of business was the salon; she had to sell it. It had been her project and child for seven years now, but the love for Kouture Kuts was gone. It bored her. She daydreamed about Miami and Omar while she styled her client's hair, changed her service days from five days a week to four, and simply wasn't as creative as she had once been. She remembered the business card of a gentleman she had met at Johnny Manana's a few months prior, and decided to give him a call about selling the salon.

She talked on the phone to Paul for almost a half hour. The first ten minutes consisted of him trying to remember who she was. The next ten minutes they talked about the salon and setting up a lunch meeting to go over the specifics.

They scheduled the dinner meeting for Thursday, and Paul had suggested The Melting Pot in Old City. Selena was more than happy about the suggestion. It was one of her favorite restaurants. Selena had enough time to go home and change after she left the salon. She wasn't set to meet Paul until 7:00 p.m. After she showered, she sat on the edge of her bed eyeing her closet, trying to figure out what to wear. She didn't want to look too sexy, but at the same time, she did want to catch an eye or two.

She decided on a cream fitted dress from bebé. It wasn't too short, but the v-cut in the back added the right amount of spice. She had the perfect pair of Stuart Weitzman gold strappy sandals that would coordinate perfectly with the dress. She walked into her bathroom to plug in her flat iron and apply her makeup. She had been wearing her hair bone straight lately, with a part down the middle. She had been thinking about going back to her golden bronze, but for now, the crimson was working wonderfully.

Her makeup and hair were flawless, and it was still

only six o'clock. She decided to call Omar. She hadn't called him since the Friday before Arielle's procedure; she had been too emotionally drained. But she missed him, and she wanted to know why he hadn't even so much as texted her. He answered on the third ring, and his deep baritone voice instantly made her smile.

"Hey honey, how are you?"

"I'm good, how are you?"

"Uhh... just been a lil' drained emotionally, the past few days, but I'm fine now. I miss you, what ya doin' this weekend?"

"I'm actually gonna be in Cali this weekend. Going to visit my brother and a few homies, a lil' homeboy getaway," he chuckled.

Selena joined in the laughter, but was really a little annoyed that she wouldn't be able to see him, and he hadn't so much as cared that she said she was emotionally drained. Selena knew Omar was still immature in a lot of ways, including sexually, but she wanted him for some reason. He made her laugh, and he was successful. She wanted the life of a millionaire's wife; she had put in her dues.

She was a college-educated entrepreneur. It was time for her to be taken care of and travel the world. Omar may not have known it, but he was the person who was going to afford her the lifestyle she wanted. After setting up a getaway to see Omar the following weekend, she hung up so she could be on her way to meet with Paul. She had to sell the salon, and quickly. Miami awaited.

* * * * *

Paul was already seated by the time Selena arrived at about 7:15. As soon as he recognized her walking towards the table, he immediately hung up his phone and stood up to greet her. He extended his arm, gently pulled her hand to his thin lips, and softly planted a tasteful kiss on her hand. She thought it was a bit old fashioned, but admired his chivalry. He was a well dressed man, black dress pants, a pea green colored shirt, and a pair of black Salvatore Ferragamo shoes. Selena noticed them because Sean had the same exact pair. He used to wear them on date nights. The two greeted each other as the waitress came over with water and menus for the duo.

He smelled edible. Selena's usual prediction of perfumes and colognes was off this evening as she spoke softly. "212 Sexy, huh?"

"That's what I remembered about when we met, you knew off hand my cologne."

They both chuckled.

"Unfortunately Ms. Nichols, you're wrong this evening," he said in a very sexy voice.

"It has to be. You know how some people are connoisseurs of music, wine, and food? That's me in fragrance and aroma, so you, Mr. Major are quite the jokester, I see."

She sipped her water and smiled at Paul.

"I admit, I have a playful personality at times, but I wouldn't fool you. It's actually L'Imperatrice, by D&G."

Selena was shocked that she was wrong. To others, it would not have been a big deal, but Selena had followed fragrance since she was a small girl. Their grandmother used to say it was because her first blanket when she was a baby was scented with her mother's favorite fragrance. The blanket was never washed, and until this day, Selena still had the blanket and the half-full bottle of Chloe that her mother had before she died. It was her grandmother's way of keeping her mother in her life.

Selena mustered up a smile. "At any rate, it smells wonderful."

That was the icebreaker needed to begin a long evening of conversation. At eleven thirty when Selena arrived home, slightly tipsy from the two glasses of wine she drank at dinner, all she could think about was taking a hot shower, spraying her bedroom with Lavender Vanilla Chamomile, and lying in bed until she fell asleep. However, all she thought about on the entire ride home, during her shower, and while lying in bed was Paul.

He was a gentleman, a businessman, and an overall nice person. Selena knew that Paul was attracted to her. Women knew that kind of thing from the very beginning. It all relied on how they decided to play it out, and Selena was unsure. He was definitely going to be her broker. Putting Kouture Kuts on the market in just a few weeks was the plan. During the conversation, Selena learned a lot about Paul. He was only 45, which was younger than she had originally thought. He wasn't just a real estate broker. He also owned four nightclubs in New York, which was where he was originally from. He had no children, traveled often, and enjoyed fine cuisine.

He would be the perfect mate if Selena wasn't in love with Omar. Omar lacked every quality that Selena liked in Paul, but he was young, flashy, physically fit, and charming. Selena's thoughts soon switched from Paul to Omar, and then finally to sleep.

* * * * *

Selena was up early on a Friday morning. Even though business had changed for Kouture Kuts, Friday was always a busy day. She had eight clients scheduled, and five of them were sew-ins. Her last client of the day would be Andrea at 5 p.m., and Selena was looking forward to it. She was the only one in her appointment book for the day that didn't require some type of hair extension or chemical treatment. Andrea sometimes irritated Selena because she asked so many questions, and always had an opinion; especially about things Selena didn't want her to have an opinion about.

She always seemed to get more information out of Selena than she liked to give. Grandma had raised Selena and Tamara to keep their business private, and Selena wasn't used to a person who was never afraid to ask a question, even about the most personal issues. She also knew that Andrea was the closest thing to family that she had right now, and it felt good every couple of weeks to have someone to talk to. She initially wasn't going to tell a soul about her plan to sell the salon, but it was burning up inside of her, and tonight over cocktails was the perfect time to disclose her plans.

By noon, Selena only had four clients remaining, and her next client wasn't scheduled until 12:30 p.m. She decided to call Omar. The phone went to voicemail after the first ring. Before she was able to leave a message, the notification for a new text message popped up. It read, *Bout to hop on this flight to L.A. Call u when I land.*

Selena smiled like a high schooler and simply responded, *I'll be waiting XOXO.* She heated up leftover spinach dip and Artisan bread from last night's dinner. She sat in her back office and ate as she daydreamed about her move to Florida. She was excited, and knew that once she was closer to Omar, their relationship would blossom into what it was supposed to be.

As soon as her last sip of iced tea was finished, she heard her buzzer ring. It was Natalie, her 12:30. She quickly washed her hands and grabbed a bottle of Bath and Body Works Lilac Blossom room spray. One thing she despised just as much as unpleasant smelling colognes and perfumes were rooms that smelled like food and garbage.

She greeted her client and began to wash her hair. This client would be a process, so Selena mentally prepared herself as she scrubbed her hair in the sink. Her hair was damaged and broken, and she wanted a full weave. She had a picture of Tyra Banks as the style choice for Selena to mimic. By a quarter until two, Selena had sewn in the last track. She wanted it long and straight, so there wasn't much left for Selena to do except cut a few layers in it and bevel out the flyaway pieces. At 2:00, the miracle was complete.

Natalie pulled out her lip-gloss and check card at the same time. Selena was big on customer service, and never believed in talking on her cell phone while she had clients, but this was an exception. Paul was calling, and she was excited to hear any information he may have regarding selling the salon and getting to Miami. She answered as she slid Natalie's card down the machine. Natalie didn't mind her taking a call. She was too engrossed in admiring her hair in the mirror. In a matter of minutes, Natalie was out the door.

Selena abruptly realized that the conversation with Paul was no longer about business. Paul was discussing them, and the chemistry he thought they had. Selena was appreciative of the honesty and enthusiasm that Paul had about Selena's character, and the positive vibes he felt about her, but she quickly changed the conversation to the business at hand.

"I enjoyed your company as well, Paul. When do you think we can put the salon on the market?"

Paul sensed a bit of annoyance in Selena's voice, and was able to shift his direction to business without the conversation turning awkward for him.

"I was hoping that in the next couple of days, we could meet up, and—"

Selena interrupted with a tad bit of annoyance, as she assumed he was still speaking in terms of a personal relationship. "Listen, I am interested in you helping to get my business sold, can we please focus on that aspect?"

"Of course, that is why I need to meet up with you at the salon. You cut me off before I could finish. I need to come do an appraisal, see how much equity you have in the salon, and research going prices for other businesses in the area."

Selena was slightly embarrassed by her brash response, but they agreed to meet on Sunday when the salon was closed.

At exactly 5:00 p.m., Andrea walked in the shop with her long hair pulled back in a ponytail. It appeared that she had been sweating for days. Her face was moist, and she was showing her abs of steel wearing a red sports bra, a pair of black yoga pants, and red and black Nike Air Max sneakers. She was obviously coming from the gym. She walked over to give Selena a hug.

She frowned and playfully opted for a high-five. "Girl please, with all that sweat."

She was glad she was so sweaty that they couldn't hug. The smell of that Paris Hilton was oozing out of her pores. She knew most people had their favorite fragrances, but was baffled as to why Andrea and Tamara opted to wear only one hideous fragrance, when there were so many other fragrance options.

Selena prompted Andrea to come back to the wash station so that she could begin.

"Come on, chica, a cocktail or two is calling my name," she said in her best impersonation of a Spanish woman.

Andrea laughed and hurried over to the sink. "So what's been up, girlfriend? How is Arielle doing?"

Selena was caught off guard by the question and instantly had a flashback of the last conversation she and her sister had. She lied in her response to Andrea.

"She's doing well, school starts next week. Hopefully, she has learned from the experience."

She quickly changed the subject. "So what's up with you and Mr. Dreadlocks?"

"Not a thing." He has no goals in life at all. I want a successful partner. Not saying he has to have it all now, but at least someone who is working towards their dreams. You know what I mean?" she said in a serious tone.

Selena agreed. Andrea was six years younger than Selena. She worked full-time as a Registrar at University of Penn Hospital, and went to school part-time to pursue her dream of becoming a registered nurse.

"I feel you Drea, it makes for a better relationship when ya'll can build together and accomplish dreams as one. That's what I miss the most about Sean. We moved as a unit and always supported each other."

"I know you do. I saw his daughter last week, she is adorable," Andrea stated nonchalantly.

Selena was startled at the statement because she never once mentioned to Andrea anything about Sean's daughter.

"Whose daughter?" she asked, just to see how much she knew.

"Sean's. Come to find out, the girl he had the baby by is friends with my cousin, Myesha, from 22nd St. Remember you did her hair a few times?"

"Oh yeah, I remember. It's a small world."

Selena turned on the sit-under dryer, waited for Andrea to be seated, and placed the hood over her head to begin her deep conditioning treatment. She walked away from the dryer and walked to her back office to grab a bottled water. She closed the door slightly to gather her thoughts. This was why Selena never cared to keep female company. Someone always knew someone and always had a story to tell, and this was something she did not want to relive.

It had only been nine months since she found out about Sean's infidelity, which had created a child and nine months since his death. She thought of Sean and his child often, but living her life and moving forward made the difficult times seem better. These types of conversations also made Selena think twice about her friendship with Andrea.

She knew that things she mentioned or talked about weren't said to deliberately upset her, but she always knew something or someone. Andrea was a social butterfly and sometimes thrived off gossip. Selena listened, and sometimes even enjoyed it, but she was never a fan of listening to gossip or hardcore facts about her own life. She took a big gulp from her Evian water bottle and gathered her composure. She didn't want Andrea to even think she was pondering what she had mentioned.

Once Andrea's hair was rinsed and blow-dried, the ladies began conversing again. "So what's up with you and Omar? You been back to Miami?"

"I haven't been in a couple of weeks, but I'm going on Friday. I miss him."

"So are ya'll official or what? I mean it's been what like five months y'all been kickin' it. No titles yet?"

Selena knew Andrea was trying to insinuate that Omar would never commit, so she figured this was the perfect time to make her aware of her upcoming plans.

"Well we aren't official, but we will be once I move to Miami!" she exclaimed.

"Whaaaaat? He asked you to move in? Now that's what I'm talking about! But wait, what about the salon? How are you gonna run the salon from Miami?" Andrea was baffled.

"I'm not. It's going on the market in a couple of weeks. I will always know how to do hair. I could open up a salon in Miami if I want. I honestly just need a break from everything; the salon, Philly, and all the memories that surround me. I mean this past year has been one hurt after the other, and Selena wants to live, be free, and find my purpose."

She stared around the salon at the wonderful decor that had once been her inspiration for living. It had now become a constant reminder of heartache.

"Well, I am happy for you, and now I'll have somewhere

to visit when I need to get away."

Selena had just sprayed Andrea's hair with a finishing gloss by Bio Silk, passed her the mirror, and snatched her purple apron off. She didn't care where they were going. She wasn't even changing her clothes. That's how bad she wanted to have a drink. Andrea still had to stop at home because she needed to shower. Selena decided to keep her car parked in the garage attached to her building and ride with Andrea. She could always stop back by afterwards or stay over at Andrea's place if she was too intoxicated to drive.

Andrea's 2004 black Honda Accord Coupe was cute, but it looked like a pigsty on the inside. There were bubble gum wrappers, a fry or two here and there, and it looked as if it hadn't been vacuumed in ages. It smelled like an old gym bag due to the various garments she had draped over the back seat. Selena was already regretting her decision not to drive and to even go out in the first place.

It wasn't ten minutes after they began to sip their first apple martinis at Z Lounge, that miraculously "dread head," which is what Selena called him, showed up. Selena was instantly annoyed. The purpose of their outing was a girl's night out to drink, eat, and talk shit about men. So why was there a man sitting at their table? After he ordered the ladies another round, he excused himself and walked over to the bar where he began talking to someone he knew.

"Damn Drea, why you ain't tell me he was coming? I could have drank at my house." Selena rolled her eyes and took another sip of her drink.

"I didn't know he was gonna pop up. He asked where I was headed to when we were at my place. I said we were coming here, but I didn't invite him."

"Unless you want a nigga to show up, you never tell him where ya goin'. Messin' up our lil' girl's night. You knew what you was doin', slick ass." Selena flagged her and finished off the rest of her martini.

Just as he walked back to the table, T. Pain's "Buy You a Drink" started to play. Selena looked over at the dance floor, admiring some of the couples she saw dancing seductively. She looked across the table and noticed Andrea and "Dread Head" pecking and fondling on each other like teenagers. She missed Sean. He loved to dance, and if he were there, she would definitely be having fun, kissing, dancing, being in love. There was absolutely nothing she could do about the love from Sean, which she missed so much. He was gone forever, and all that remained were memories. She felt herself getting emotional and quickly pulled herself together. Besides, she had a plan. In a few months, she would be in Miami claiming her man, Omar.

She woke up on Andrea's couch at about 8 a.m. She felt horrible. The last thing she remembered was her fifth apple martini. She walked down the hallway to Andrea's bathroom and noticed that her bedroom door was closed. She knew she had company. She went into the bathroom and pulled her toiletry bag out of her oversized Louis Vuitton purse. She brushed her teeth, used an Oil of Olay Foaming Facewash wipe, brushed her hair back into a ponytail, glided some Bobbi Brown Lip Smoother, and was ready to go. She decided not to interrupt whatever could be going on in Andrea's room. Besides, she could catch the train downtown and stop in Sephora before picking up her car from the salon.

Sephora was the next best thing to heaven for Selena.

Each fragrance represented a different personality. Daisy was the fragrance she loved when she felt flirty and sassy, Miss Dior Cherie when she felt adventurous and spontaneous, Viva La Juicy when she felt like a queen and wanted to be catered to, and Balenciaga when she wanted to be wild. She walked through the store for almost thirty minutes, smelling different fragrances. Some made her smile inside and out, and others made her stomach turn.

She decided on Princess by Vera Wang. When she inhaled, the aroma put her in Miami on the beach, enjoying a lunch date with her husband Omar Henderson as the paparazzi snapped pictures. She walked out of the store, black and white bag dangling, in a great mood. She couldn't wait to go home, shower and feel the droplets of fragrance fall on her neck. She needed her bed.

Selena wanted to feel pretty, tonight; not for any man, but for herself. She was feminine in all ways, and always thought women should be sexy and smell pleasant at all times, not just before a hot date. While searching in her closet for the Agent Provacateur nightgown that Omar had bought her last month, she stumbled across the box. It was a pink, round box that actually looked like a hat box. Over the years, the color had faded, and the pink was now pastel and resembled an Easter egg. In the box was the prettiest pink and white knitted blanket. It was worn out and frilled at the ends, but Selena looked at it as if it were brand new.

She held it up to her face and inhaled as the tears fell from her eyes. She still smelled the Chloe perfume. She glanced down at the bottle that was also lying in the box, and wondered what her mother was like. She had heard plenty of stories from her grandmother, but after Tamara had painted a whole other picture of their mother, Selena was confused. Tamara had taken care of Selena her entire life, but she had also lied to her. Could she have really been this deceitful, loose woman that Tamara described? She had longed all her life just to touch her mother's face, but now, she wanted to forget and to never become what she was.

Selena removed the perfume from the box and placed it on her dresser. She put the blanket back in the box and closed it tightly. She put her robe and slippers on, grabbed the box, and began to walk downstairs. She stopped in the kitchen and grabbed her tall lighter out of the drawer. She normally used it to light her grill, but she would be using it in a different manner tonight. She sprinkled the box with some lighter fluid and ignited it into a small campfire sized blaze. She stood emotionless as the box disintegrated.

She didn't know much about her life anymore from all the lies and deception, but she knew she didn't want anything to do with it. She was a different woman than her sister, mother, and grandmother. She said a prayer for her niece. She loved Arielle, but knew she wasn't in control of what their relationship would be. She trusted in God with it. As the fire began to slow down, Selena went in the house and grabbed some water to help extinguish the flames. She felt free and over the pain. Her move would be the icing on the cake.

CHAPTER 8

It was only the first week of September, and this particular Sunday morning was a bit brisk. Selena wanted to sleep in, but had a 10:00 meeting with Paul at the salon. After her shower and her three sprays of her new Vera Wang fragrance, she pulled a green PINK sweat suit out of the closet, and an all-white pair of Nike Air Max. She pulled her hair up into a neat bun, glossed her pouty lips, and was on her way to begin the process of starting her new life.

The fall-like breeze felt amazing as Selena drove down South Street looking for a parking spot near Starbucks. Her phone rang while she was getting back in her vehicle. She looked at the number. It was Paul, of course. She smiled because she liked his punctuality, and sure enough, he was calling to let her know that he would be pulling up in about five minutes. This was perfect, because it was 9:50, and Selena was about five minutes away from the salon, herself.

She walked in the salon, coffee in hand, looking around at what used to be her passion. It still baffled her that she no longer had the love for it that she once had. It seemed almost as if her love for the salon died with Sean. Before she was able to become emotional, Paul knocked on the door.

Selena turned and instantly smiled. He was dressed casually in a burnt orange button down Polo shirt, dark blue jeans, and a pair of chocolate brown Louis Vuitton sneaker boots. Selena was impressed with his sense of style, for an older man. He walked in and greeted her with a kiss on her hand and the wonderful aroma of his Burberry Touch cologne tickled her nose. He complimented how beautiful her face looked with her hair pulled up, and began to walk around the salon.

He admired the decor and the quality tiling and window treatments that made the salon look very high-end. From the salon chairs, to the antique style wash basins aligned along the back wall of the posh salon, it was definitely top notch. After a thorough walk through, inside and out, Paul was ready to talk business.

"Well Ms. Nichols, you have a prime piece of property on your hands. Location, fixtures, you've got it all. If we were putting your property on the market today, we could easily list it at $265,000.00."

"Really?" she asked.

Selena was amazed. Seven years ago, she purchased the property for only $120,000.00 in a buy-as-is deal. Sean and some of his friends did all of the fix-up work the property required. There were so many heartfelt sentiments in every piece of tile that was laid, and every swipe of paint on the walls. Selena knew that in order for her to progress and be entirely happy in life, this was a step she had to take.

"Let's do it."

* * * * *

Friday night couldn't come fast enough. Selena daydreamed all day on Wednesday about hopping on the plane and arriving in Miami to see Omar again. She had just gotten off the phone with him and confirmed that she would be in town for the weekend. This made her even more excited. She wanted to lay in his king sized bed and be held. She needed him, and she was willing to wait until he was ready to fully commit.

In the midst of her thoughts, her cell phone rang and it was Paul. She wondered if he had good news about the salon, and eagerly answered on the first ring.

Paul never mentioned the salon in the conversation. Instead, he mentioned an upcoming trip to New York City to close out a deal. Initially, Selena was bored and wanted him to get to the point. She had no clue why he would call her to talk about a property he was closing on. Just before she was about to rudely interrupt Paul and end the conversation, he mentioned something that caught Selena's attention. Paul was selling the clubs he owned in New York. He was over the party scene, and was ready to enjoy life and travel. The nightclubs had begun to be too overwhelming, and he was closing the deal next week in New York.

Paul wanted to know if she wanted to accompany him to the closing. She was hesitant at first, but thought it would only help her to learn about the process, and it was a free trip to New York. She agreed, and let him know that she was going to visit a friend in Miami for the weekend and would be returning on Tuesday morning.

Selena was excited. Her life was beginning to change

for the better. Soon, the salon would be no more, and her only responsibility would be to enjoy life. She inhaled the Japanese cherry blossom scented oil that sat in a vase of artificial flowers on the receptionist desk at the salon, turned the lights off, and closed the doors.

The flight to Miami seemed longer than usual. Selena was the first passenger standing once the plane came to a complete stop. She grabbed her carry on Kate Spade duffel bag and scurried off the plane. She turned her cell phone on to call Omar and let him know she had arrived. She called his number and got no answer. She waited a few moments and tried again.

He answered on the third ring and told her to catch a cab to his place.

She thought for sure that he had originally said he would pick her up, but she didn't feel like arguing. She just wanted to see him. She hopped in a cab and was at his condo in about twenty-five minutes. She paid the cab driver and treated her lips to a swipe of M·A·C lip glass. She applied a dab of Clinique's "happy" body lotion to her hands for the mood she intended to be in during her stay this weekend in Miami, and forever, once everything was taken care of.

She arrived on the tenth floor and rang the bell to Omar's condo. He opened the door, but to Selena's surprise, he didn't appear excited. His hug was weak, and his skin was cold and without a scent. No cologne, soap, laundry detergent, not even sweat. Selena tried to warm him up by dropping her bag and immediately kissing all over Omar, pushing him back on his couch and straddling over him like a jockey.

His response was initially little to none, but once he

felt her wetness, he quickly responded by sliding his stiff manhood inside of her. She stared at Omar's perfectly chiseled face as he held his head back on the couch, with his eyes closed, trying hard to hold in his deep moans. Their intimate session only lasted about five minutes before Omar grabbed her ass tightly and thrust himself deeper into her walls of lust. He was sweaty and satisfied.

Selena hadn't reached her climax with Omar since they first started seeing each other. She hoped that eventually he would take the time to learn her and please her completely. He was young, and she knew she had to teach him how to handle her.

She walked over to her bag, grabbed a small box from it, and passed it to Omar. He slowly opened it and gave a small smirk. It was a bottle of "Unforgivable" by Sean Jean.

"Let's get a shower, so you can spray some on before we go grab something to eat."

"The shower part sounds great, but I really don't feel much like going out. I could easily get someone to go pick us up some Phillipe's, and we can relax and enjoy each other's company," he said as he gently stroked her face.

Initially, Selena wasn't sold on the staying in idea, but Omar was being so affectionate. He seemed like he missed her so much, that lying in bed and spending time with him was the only thing that mattered.

They enjoyed a feast of Peking Duck, Lobster Fried Rice, and Calamari Salad, while sipping on Moscato. Selena thought the timing was perfect to start a conversation on her plans to move to Miami.

"So are you excited about the upcoming season?" she asked, while lying on his chest.

"Of course, I mean, it's work, so I'm enjoying the time off now, but I'm ready. Practice has already begun, that's why I'm so tired. Been chillin' too hard the last couple of months. The first preseason game is October 13th I think, so right around the corner."

"So when you're on the road for work, how often are you in Miami?"

"Only when we have home games, which is probably once or twice a week. The schedule is pretty hectic."

"That is hectic. How would you feel about having someone here for you when you are at home?" she asked nervously.

Omar hesitated. The question had caught him off guard. When he finally responded, it wasn't the excitement that Selena had hoped for.

"You mean you living here? I mean, I've never lived with a female. Not sure I'm ready for that. We are still getting to know each other and..."

Selena cut him off, realizing where the conversation was going. Omar held her chin up and began to backpedal his answer because her feelings were obviously hurt. It was clear that he wasn't ready for a committed relationship, but he did have feelings for Selena and never liked to see her upset.

"I mean living together, I'm not ready. But if you chose to move to Florida, how could I be mad at that?"

Selena began to smile and wrapped her arms tightly around his neck. That was all she needed to hear. Once she got back to Philly, Paul had to get on his job with the salon. She was Miami bound, and nothing could stop her.

The rest of the weekend flew by, and before she knew it, she was right back at Philadelphia International. This time it was different. She was on cloud nine, ready to begin looking for a condo close to the beach, and close to Omar.

She walked into her townhouse and made her way to her bedroom where she fell backwards on to her bed. She remembered that she would be traveling to New York with Paul the next day, and wanted to go through her closet to find the perfect outfit.

While looking through the closet, her sense of smell took over her mind. She thought of Sean and the times they had made love in this house. She smelled his Angel cologne throughout the entire closet and bedroom. It was driving her crazy. She missed her first love; she would do anything to hold him one more time. Thinking of Sean, his scent embedded in her mind, she realized that not only did she have to sell the salon, she had to sell their home. As much as she was ready to move on, she knew it would be hard.

Selena picked up the phone to call Paul to confirm that they were still on for New York the next day, and to mention putting her house up for sale as well. She smiled as she hung up the phone. All of the plans were still in order, and upon their arrival back to Philadelphia, he would get everything ready to put the house on the market.

It was already 8:00 a.m., and Selena and Paul were set to meet in Center City by 10:00. She was showered and smelling absolutely delicious in her favorite fragrance, Emilio Pucci. She stepped into her charcoal gray Juicy Couture dress that fit her athletic physique like a glove. It was the perfect combination of professional and sexy. The gray Belle pumps with zipper accents gave the outfit the extra punch it needed to send Selena into the fashion elite of the Big Apple. Her bouncy crimson curls created a beautiful accent to the gray dress, along with her clutch bag that was the same color as her hair. By 9:30, she was out the door and on her way to meet Paul.

Paul texted her and directed her to park her car in the lot at Liberty Place, which was where his office was located. She waited in the lot where he asked her to as a black Suburban, looking like the President was on the inside, pulled up beside her.

At first, she paid no attention to it. She thought for sure Paul would be pulling up in his Mercedes for their journey to New York. After a few minutes, the rear driver's side window slowly began to come down. Paul leaned his perfectly trimmed salt and pepper head out of the window with a hearty smile.

"Good morning, beautiful. Are you going to join me?"

"Well, I thought you'd never ask."

She smiled as she walked on the other side of the truck, followed closely by the driver who opened the door for her.

She climbed in and was greeted with a warm smile, kiss on the hand, and the pleasant aroma of Dolce & Gabana's "The One." The scent made Selena smile instantly. She went beyond the smile and kiss on the hand. She leaned over and gave Paul a long, tight hug. She had to catch herself, as she almost began to run her hands up and down his back. They both gently pulled away at the same time and sat quietly for a few moments.

Paul broke the silence by asking Selena if she wanted to stop and have breakfast, or if she had eaten already.

"I'm actually not hungry. Maybe just some coffee or tea, thank you."

Paul nodded in agreement and let the driver know to stop at the next Starbucks.

The ride to New York was informative. Selena was able to fully understand how Paul had become so wealthy. It began with an inheritance that was left to him by his grandfather. He explained how he obtained his broker's license and began to purchase properties to renovate and re-sell in order to maintain a stable income. When one of the homes sold for almost two million dollars about ten years ago, he quickly went into business with some old college friends and purchased his first night club.

The club did well, however, his business partners were content with the lifestyle they were blessed with. They did not desire the risk of obtaining more nightclubs, as Paul did. After two years in business together, they bought out his partnership, and Paul was free to purchase the two other nightclubs he was interested in. The two become four in about two additional years, and he had maintained four classy, respectable establishments in the Manhattan area ever since.

He was now ready to relax and enjoy life. He spoke of how he never took the time to commit to a real relationship because he was too focused on making his life comfortable. Now at forty-five, he was more than ready to settle down with the perfect someone.

Selena admired his ambition and his candid conversations about his life, but she knew she wasn't attracted to Paul physically. Whenever his aroma made her mind drift towards the possibility of him being more than a mentor, she looked at his gray hair that lay perfectly brushed atop his head as a reminder that he was not for her.

They arrived at the Mandarin Oriental Hotel in

Manhattan and sat quietly in a small conference room. There was coffee, tea, and a variety of fruits and pastries on the table. No more than two minutes after they arrived, two men walked into the room– one older and one younger. Paul stood and shook each of their hands and introduced Selena as his assistant. Selena was flattered, and the four sat at the table getting acquainted before the older gentleman, Harry Simpson, was ready to get down to business.

The two men were father and son, Harry and Christopher Carbone, apparently two of the biggest property and club owners in New York City. They smelled like money, Paco Rabanne's "One Million" cologne to be exact. Selena didn't know which of the two men was wearing the intoxicating fragrance, but she assumed it was the young handsome son. He was tall, with dark hair and stunning brown eyes. His skin tone was deep and olive, and with the last name, he had to be of Italian descent.

He and Selena made constant eye contact throughout the meeting. She wasn't really paying attention to the details of the meeting until she heard the amount of money involved. Paul had just signed the paperwork. It was official. He was no longer the owner of Lavish Lounge, Dreams Gentleman Club and Lounge, and Club Xtacy. He was now the recipient of 3.5 million dollars in exchange for them.

Selena couldn't believe it. She maintained her cool while still in the company of the Carbones, but hi-fived Paul and gave him a huge hug the moment they walked out the door. Selena had never been a female to worry about what a man had. She always took care of herself. What she and Sean had attained, they did it together. But this was different. She wasn't in a committed relationship, and she had a desire for everything she never thought twice about.

In the midst of the hug, the intoxicating aroma of Paul's cologne made her body twinge with pleasure. She held him tightly and began to rub her hands up and down his back with her nose pressed deeply into his chest, becoming high off his scent. Paul responded affectionately, gliding his hands down to her firm bottom and gripping it with the right amount of roughness and tenderness. He lifted her chin and began to kiss her gently across her full lips.

Selena thought to pull away, but the kiss felt so warm and real. She closed her eyes tightly and leaned her head back so that Paul could kiss her neck. She was moist, and she wanted Paul. The realization that they were still in the conference room was a complete turn on. She grabbed Paul by the waist of his pants and walked ahead of him. Paul knew what that meant.

Conveniently, there was already a room reserved for Paul. Selena smirked when she realized that Paul had planned to stay the afternoon in New York. At that point, with him already being financially secure, and now closing the deal on 3.5 million dollars, she didn't mind at all. She wanted to give him whatever he desired.

Room #306 was grand, with a beautiful view and fresh flowers all over the room. Selena undressed as Paul stood by the bed in amazement. After she was completely naked, she began to kiss Paul and undress him at the same time. In no time, they both stood naked, caressing each other wildly. Selena gently pushed Paul on the bed so that she could climb on top of him. She was ready, and his gray hair and semi-flabby belly didn't matter.

Before she inserted his stiff penis into her wet walls, she opened her mouth wide and began to twirl her tongue around the head of his above average sized manhood. Paul could barely contain himself. He moaned and gripped Selena's hair while she slid her mouth and hands up and down. He grabbed her hair harder and pulled her toward him. He was ready to feel her.

She climbed up and gently placed Paul inside of her. They started off slowly, but the aroma of the fresh flowers and Paul's cologne was turning Selena into an animal. She clinched her love muscles tightly as she slid up and down. Paul held her butt and began to gently kiss her breasts. Selena was hot and began to shake. She knew she was almost at her climax, but wanted to be sure Paul was able to be satisfied as well.

She leaned forward and began moaning and licking his ear. Paul moved his hands up her back and dug his manicured nails in. He then let out a deep moan, and Selena knew he was satisfied. Right after Paul's release, Selena's vagina began to throb and melted all over Paul's semi-hard penis.

When Paul and Selena woke up, it was well into evening, almost 8 o'clock. As much as Selena wanted to stay, the salon wasn't sold yet, and she did have a business to run. She looked over at a sleeping Paul. Although they had indulged in some of the best sex she'd had in quite a while, at this moment, she wasn't attracted to him. His body was square, and he had absolutely no muscle tone. It wasn't what she was used to.

She wasn't sure who she was becoming. Paul's money was attractive to her, and she didn't know why. That was the moment she understood why she was so attracted to Omar, even with his lack of commitment, lack luster bedroom performance, and childish behavior.

Omar and Paul were the perfect combination of a man. One sexy, wealthy, with a great sense of humor; and the other, a gentleman who knew how to please a lady, stable, and able to make a woman desire him with something as small as wearing cologne. The two of them together were why she missed Sean. Although Sean had been deceitful and created a child, she couldn't help but imagine what life would be like for her now if she hadn't gone to Jamaica with Tamara and if he hadn't been killed. Before she could become too emotional, Paul opened his eyes and reached out to Selena.

"Hello, beautiful. That was an awesome way to wake up… to your face."

Selena smiled and laid her head on his chest as she felt a tear about to drop due to her thoughts prior to Paul waking up. He kissed her on her forehead and invited her to a shower together before they headed back to PA. The shower was wonderful. Selena couldn't believe the amount of pleasure Paul delivered for his age. Paul had some gourmet sandwiches delivered for the ride home. The two lay in each other's arms the entire time.

Once Selena was in her X5 on her way to her town home, she daydreamed, wondering if what she sought was right here, versus in Florida. Life was beginning to become complicated again, but she was going to handle it with grace this time around. She was going to live and let the pieces fall where they may. She didn't know if she was supposed to pursue Omar, or build a life with Paul. Whatever the answer was, she would find out soon.

CHAPTER 9

The next few weeks at the salon were pretty routine, aside from the fact that Selena had been out with Paul just about every night since New York. They dined at the best restaurants, took spontaneous trips to Atlantic City, and they had even gone on a few shopping sprees. On one, Paul had purchased Selena a $3000.00 Oscar de la Renta gown. There was an upcoming gala in New York City that would honor various business owners and self-made entrepreneurs. Paul was a guest of honor. Selena was thrilled. She hadn't been anywhere that she had to wear a gown to since her prom. Second to what would have been her wedding day, she couldn't wait to put the dress on and become a living doll for the evening.

She had spoken to Omar at least two times a week lately, but neither of them had mentioned anything about seeing each other. She was fine with that. Selena was enjoying this time away from Omar, and she hoped he was missing her. He needed to show her a sign that he wanted her for more than a companion once a month. Besides, she was really enjoying the connection between her and Paul. Other than his awkward build, he was the perfect man with plenty of money to spend on a young thang like Selena.

Tonight, she and Paul would be staying in at his home in Ambler, Pa. Since they had started seeing each other, neither had been to the other's home. They always met at mutual locations. Tonight would be different. Paul was cooking, and Selena was eagerly in route once she locked the salon doors.

Her navigation system led her directly to the driveway of 830 Tennis Avenue, and Selena was simply amazed. The cabin style mini-mansion looked cozy and elegant, at the same time. She pulled in the driveway and began to walk up the lit walkway to the front door of the home. Paul answered and greeted her with a kiss. The smell of fresh seafood filled the air as Selena admired the beautifully finished wood floors. The decor was simple, yet elegant, and the natural earth tones were the featured colors throughout the home.

"Your home is beautiful."

"Thank you, but it's nowhere near as beautiful as you are."

Paul was good for corny little lines, but they always made Selena smile.

Her phone rang as they sat in the living room having a few cocktails before dinner. It was Omar. She debated in her head whether she should answer or not. On the fourth ring, she picked up and tried to act as normal as possible. Even though she and Paul weren't an official couple, she didn't want to him to feel uncomfortable at all.

"Hello," she answered, nervously smiling at Paul at the same time.

"Hey lady, what's up with you?"

"I'm good and you?" She lowered her voice and began to walk around the house while talking to Omar.

"I'm gonna be in town tomorrow night. We're playing ya hometown, them bum ass Sixers. I wanna see you."

Chuckling at his comment, Selena responded, "Whatever nigga. Alright, well just call me when you get here, and we will meet up."

"Cool, but why you rushing me off the phone? You busy?"

Selena was flattered by his attempt to care about talking or spending time with her. It was rare with Omar. He rarely showed affection, or interest for that matter.

"No, not busy per se, but I am in the middle of dinner." She was hoping to get another response, even one of jealousy.

"Say no more, I'll hit you up tomorrow."

That was the story of Selena and Omar. As soon as she thought he cared and thought of her as more than just someone to pass time with, he always had to mess it up. It was perfectly fine with Selena though, because tonight belonged to Mr. Paul Major. The stuffed salmon, sautéed shrimp, and fresh broccoli he had prepared were just an appetizer to the meal of a woman Selena was prepared to serve him.

* * * * *

Selena and Andrea didn't get to the game until almost halftime. Neither of them knew anything about basketball, but the courtside seats and stares from everyone wondering who's special guests they were, made up for what they considered to be the most boring sport. The pair sat and cheered each time a player on the Miami Heat scored a basket, especially Omar, which drew awkward stares from the hometown crowd.

"So girl, what is going on with your move to Miami and all? I know you ain't takin' that old nigga serious. This is your life right here, it's so you, Leen. I mean, I know dude has some money, but I know it ain't no Omar Henderson kinda money."

"You are crazy. I would love this, but I don't know. It just seems so forced with Omar. He plays games, like he ain't ready sometimes. I like attention, affection, and to feel needed. His young ass gets arrogant sometimes, that's that Leo shit. Like I keep telling you, Paul is older, but don't get it twisted, he knows how to make a woman feel like a woman."

"If you say so, girl."

After the game, Selena and Andrea waited for Omar in a secluded room where an escort had taken them. It was nearly an hour after the game before Omar came walking through the door. He spoke to Andrea and walked over to Selena and kissed her on the forehead. He smelled of soap, but no distinct aroma. She was turned off by it, but it still felt good to be held by him.

"Good game playboy, what we getting into tonight?"

"Thank you, sexy. I'm actually going to Plush Lounge, I believe, for the after party."

"Why didn't you tell me? I'm not dressed for the club."

Andrea quickly jumped in the conversation. "Me either," she said with an attitude.

They both turned and looked at Andrea, then burst into laughter.

"Well, just go back to my hotel and wait for me. I'm not staying long."

This was exactly what frustrated Selena with Omar.

He never wanted to be out with her. She had had enough.

"It's cool, O, thanks for inviting us to the game. Call me when you are through playin' games. I'm worth more than just layin' up in a hotel room, waiting on a nigga to come in."

She walked out with Andrea right behind. Omar didn't try to stop her, and she didn't look back.

* * * * *

It had been almost six months since both her salon and home had been placed on the market. Selena was becoming discouraged, and rethinking the plans she had originally made. She still talked to Omar about once a week, but hadn't seen him since the game a few months back. She and Paul were still going strong, and every time she tried to think of a reason not to be with him, he did something to make her fall deeper. Selena had made up her mind. If the salon didn't sell within three months, she was simply going to hire staff to work and take over her book. She was also going to give Omar one more test. She would go down for a week and observe him, then finally decide whether a move out of state was the right decision.

Tonight was the Urban League's Annual Gala, and the red Oscar de la Renta gown was beautiful. It had one strap, a low cut back, and huge bow accent that daintily hung from the side of the floor length gown. Her now dark brown hair was styled like her favorite era of time, the 40's. She had huge curls that were pinned ever so gently to the sides and back of her head, creating a look of waves. Her neck was bare except for the aroma of Chantecaille perfume that Paul gently dabbed on her.

He inhaled the smell of island gardenias and whispered in her ear. "You look amazing, and you smell even better."

That was a compliment far more meaningful to Selena than being told she was beautiful. Her scents represented her, and Paul made her feel loved. He knew exactly how to kiss her, hold her, and most importantly, make her feel like a woman. Tonight would be her and Paul's night to shine. She knew she looked radiant and couldn't wait to arrive and steal the attention.

The corner of Broad Street that housed The Ritz Carlton Hotel was lit up this evening. Every luxury vehicle you could imagine was in line to valet park. Selena had butterflies in her stomach as the valet walked over to her door to let her out. She stood modelesque as she waited for Paul to come around and take her arm. She gazed at the scenery and was amazed at the nightlife in the city on this warm spring night. The hustle and bustle and the elegance of the other attendees walking in the front doors of one of the most posh hotels of the city were intoxicating. Before long, Paul had extended his arm, kissed her hand, and gently begun to lead his woman to the affair.

Selena felt proud to be in a setting with so many educated, accomplished, and respected business men and women of color. Paul stood out like a sore thumb, not due to his attire; he was sharp in his Ralph Lauren all-black Tuxedo, and black Ferragamo shoes. He stood out because of his color. To look at him, most would believe he was a white man, as Selena had originally thought. He was of mixed race. His father was African American, and his mother, Italian. Paul was the spitting image of his uncle Giovanni, his mother's brother. Regardless of his race, he was a key part in tonight's event, and Selena was honored to be in his company.

The men and the women at the event all looked exquisite. Floor length gowns, and up dos were a hit for the ladies, however, Selena knew by far that she was the belle of the ball. Paul was making his rounds, introducing Selena to any and every one who would listen. The guests were respectful, and Selena felt like a queen.

She excused herself from Paul. She wanted to be sure her hair and makeup were still intact. She smiled at herself in the powder room mirror, applied a bit more lipstick, and made her way back to the ballroom to her loving Paul. She noticed Paul immediately. He was engaged in conversation with a woman whose back was turned to Selena. Selena walked towards the two with grace. The last thing she wanted anyone to think, was that she was insecure. She knew she was beautiful, and no woman could steal the attention she always received from Paul.

As she got closer, she turned her nose up at the unpleasant, yet familiar aroma that assaulted her nose. It was loud, excessive, and it almost made her nauseous. It was Lolita Lempicka, and the woman was Tamara.

The sisters stared at each other without emotion while Paul introduced them.

"This is Tamara Styles, the woman who brought my visions to life in my home, and this is Selena Nichols, the woman who has brought a smile to my heart."

He gently kissed Selena on her forehead.

It was easy to understand why Paul wouldn't think the two were related. Selena was petite and of a lighter complexion. Tamara, built like a coke bottle, and was a darker complexion. Tamara hadn't used the last name Nichols in years. She had adopted the name of her interior design company.

"Nice to meet you," Selena responded with a fake smile on her face.

"Really, are you serious, Selena? Nice to meet you? You've really selected a winner, Paul. I'm gonna excuse myself because this is neither the time nor place," she mumbled just loud enough for Paul and Selena to hear.

Paul stood confused as he watched Tamara walk away in her stunning gold evening gown. Selena turned the other way. She couldn't bear to watch her sister walk away again. Before Paul could turn around, she was marching off in the opposite direction. Paul called out for Selena once. When she didn't respond, he let her continue on. As much as he wanted her to turn around and come back, he was not about to make a spectacle of himself, or her.

It was eleven o'clock when Paul departed. Once he was in the vehicle, he immediately called Selena. She didn't answer. He gave his driver Selena's address and was on his way. In the meantime, he decided to call Tamara and see if he could get answers from her. She answered on the second ring, but didn't greet him. She knew what he wanted and just let him talk.

Once Paul was finished questioning Tamara, she let him know everything, from Selena being her half-sister, to her taking her daughter to get an abortion without her consent. Paul was in shock. He couldn't understand why in their deepest conversations, Selena had never mentioned that she had a sister.

By the time he arrived at Selena's home, he had heard an earful from Tamara and needed to talk to Selena. He wanted to know what else she could be hiding. He had developed strong feelings for Selena, and before he could move forward with what they had, he needed to know she was true. He wanted desperately for Selena to have all the right answers to his questions; he just wanted her to open up to him. He loved her.

He rang the bell and waited patiently for Selena to answer the door, but she never did. He called her phone numerous times, and listened as it went automatically to voicemail. He was hurt and worried. It was not like Selena to ignore calls and to be dishonest. He thought his judgment of her being a true person was correct. He was obviously wrong. After ringing the bell, circling the perimeter of the house just to be sure she wasn't harmed, and calling repeatedly for almost a half an hour, he hopped back in the SUV and directed the driver to take him home.

* * * * *

At the same time Paul was pulling off from in front of her door, Selena was boarding a flight to North Carolina. She had called Omar on her cab ride home from the ball. She really needed someone to talk to, and Andrea hadn't answered. Surprisingly, he answered on the first ring and sounded excited to hear from her. She initially wanted to tell him why she was upset and seek some comforting words, but the joy in his voice instantly cheered her up and she wanted to see him. He explained that they had just arrived in North Carolina, and he was on his way to his hotel room. He said that the game wasn't until the following afternoon.

Selena was delighted, and immediately hinted around to her coming to see him. He agreed, and when Selena reached home, she had enough time to log on to her computer to find a flight, change out of her gown, and throw a couple of outfits in her overnight bag.

Selena arrived at her destination at almost 2 a.m. Her hair and makeup were too much once she had taken off her gown and slid on a pair of jeans, fitted t-shirt, and a pair of brown Jeffrey Campbell sandals. She didn't even care. She had to get away.

She knew there would be a time that she would see her sister again, but she wasn't ready for it. Not at the gala, and not through Paul. She almost felt a tear drop as she looked at her phone, at the numerous calls she had ignored from Paul. She knew he loved her, but she had so much going on, and so much hurt inside of her. She didn't know what to do. She opted for the easy way out tonight. Forget about it, and spend time with the man she wished would give her half as much attention as Paul.

Omar had just gotten out the shower when Selena arrived. His white towel was wrapped around his waist when he opened the door, and his chiseled stomach held onto tiny droplets of water. He leaned his 6'4" frame down to kiss Selena on the lips and gently closed the door behind her. Again, Omar smelled of fresh soap, but still no cologne. She asked him where the one she had gotten him was.

"At home, I don't bring all of that with me. What's with you and the whole cologne thing anyway?"

Selena was startled by the question. No one had ever asked her that. People were usually taken by surprise that she knew most fragrances off the top of her head.

"I just love perfumes, colognes, and fragrance…" She stopped briefly because she was getting emotional. "My Nana said it was because, before my mother died, she had sprayed her favorite perfume on my blanket. That's all I could ever relate it to." Selena hung her head down so that Omar wouldn't see that she was near tears.

She waited for a comforting hug from Omar. Although it wasn't her complete past, this was more about her past than she had revealed to anyone since Sean, and she needed to be held.

Instead of hugging her, Omar nodded in agreement and said, "That makes sense."

Selena couldn't believe that she had just shared a part of her life with Omar that was sacred, and got nothing in return. North Carolina was beginning to feel like a mistake. She even missed Paul.

Omar stepped into his all-white Polo underwear, swiped deodorant under his arms, and sat down on the king sized bed. Selena was exhausted and couldn't stop thinking of Paul and Tamara. She *knew* Omar would be ready to be intimate, and Lord knows she didn't feel like it, but she went along with it anyway. The whole time, she silently repeated to herself that this would be the last time.

She was tired of the games with Omar. He wasn't ready to commit. He was still young. She longed for Paul, but knew she had a lot of explaining to do when she got back home. Omar fell fast asleep after he reached his climax. No hugs, kisses, or affection. Selena knew it was over and lay in bed all night next to a man she no longer desired.

She finally opened her eyes at almost eleven a.m. She hadn't even heard Omar leave. She turned over and noticed he had left money on the nightstand. Although it appeared to be a significant amount, this was one more reason why Selena knew she had to leave him alone. She went into the bathroom to take a quick shower. She needed to get on the next flight back to Philadelphia.

She thought about leaving the money on the nightstand, but quickly changed her mind and placed the stack of one hundred dollar bills in her caramel-colored Michael Kors hobo bag. Her telephone was completely dead, because in the rush of trying to get to North Carolina, she had forgotten her charger. Now she was in a mad dash to get back and try to make amends with Paul.

By three thirty in the afternoon, Selena was boarding a flight. Her mind was made up, yet she was nervous about how Paul would feel. She leaned her head back, ready to enjoy a nice 3 hour nap on her flight.

Once she arrived at home, she headed straight upstairs to her bedroom to put her Blackberry on the charger. She needed to contact Paul, but in the meantime she needed to take a hot bath and figure out what she was going to say to him. Paul had been nothing but a gentleman to her, and she couldn't believe she was jeopardizing it with someone as immature as Omar.

Once her phone came on, she had four missed calls. Two from Paul, one from Andrea, and one from a number she didn't recognize. As she slowly slid into her bath water, the smell of Jasmine bubbles tickled her nose and made her smile instantly. She held onto her cell phone tightly, being careful not to let it touch the water. She figured she would call Andrea first, not only to catch up, but to establish her alibi for when she was ready to call Paul.

Andrea answered on the third ring sounding like death.

"Well damn, what's wrong with you?"

"I have strep throat. I was calling you to cancel our lunch we had planned for today. I don't even want to think about swallowing anything."

Selena was happy she was sick. She had forgotten about their plans anyway, and she knew she would need the next few days to make things right with Paul.

"Awww I hope you feel better, Drea. My mouth was all set for those sweet potato pancakes." Selena rolled her eyes to the top of her head.

"I know right, but let me lay back down. My throat is killing me, and I have a fever."

"Alright Drea, if you need me, call me."

"Thanks," she whispered.

She sat her phone on the side of the tub briefly while she ran her fluffy body sponge up and down her arms. She was tense all over. She needed a full body massage, a bottle of champagne, and the smell of one of Paul's manly aromas in her nose to feel relaxed.

She opened her eyes when she heard the vibration of her cell phone. She glanced over and noticed it was the same number from the earlier missed call. She pressed the answer button and was surprised by who was on the phone.

She immediately stood up and grabbed her bathrobe so that she could plug her phone back up. It hadn't charged long before she got in the bathtub, and she didn't want the phone to lose battery, especially not with Tamara on the line.

Selena sat on her bed and listened to her sister's voice. She could barely concentrate on what she was saying because this was the voice that prior to Saturday night, she hadn't heard in months. The voice of the person who raised her, taught her about the birds and bees, how to carry herself like a woman, and also the voice that had lied to her since the day she was born.

Her emotions changed frequently throughout the conversation from happiness to anger. She listened to Tamara talk for almost ten minutes, initially about Paul's concern for her whereabouts. She eventually spoke on how hurt she was at the gala, and even back to her lying about Carl and how betrayed she felt when Selena had taken Arielle to get the abortion.

Selena's eyes began to fill with tears once she heard the emotions in Tamara's voice. She knew she was crying. She suggested that Tamara come over so they could talk. Tamara declined the invitation, stating that she had clients to meet with and that they could possibly get together later in the week.

Selena acted as if she were okay with the idea, but really felt that if she was extending an offer to try and at least talk about things, her clients could have waited. All that was gained from the conversation, was that she knew Paul was worried about her and that she and her sister were still a long way from being reunited, if at all.

The bathtub wasn't even an option any longer. She released the water and sat back on her bed and dialed Paul's number. Her heart raced like a horse in the Kentucky Derby while the phone rang. She felt sweaty and nervous, but instantly felt calm once he answered the phone. Selena felt awful lying to Paul and telling him that she was with Andrea "clearing her mind" instead of telling him the truth. She knew she had already hurt him enough, by not telling him about her sister and by leaving him at the party. He didn't need to be told about her trip to see Omar, because it was her last one.

She was ready to be with Paul regardless of his age, body type, or what anyone else thought. Paul was happy to hear from Selena, but he definitely let her know that he was upset that she felt she had to keep anything from him, and also that she ignored the concern that he had shown over the past two days since the gala.

He was smitten by Selena, and knew that he wanted to be with her. Unless she had decided otherwise, even the secrets she held from him prior to Saturday couldn't keep him away from her.

She changed the subject once Paul began to speak of her and Tamara ironing out their differences. She knew that it was something that she wanted to happen, but on her terms. Especially after she had just invited her sister over to talk about it all, and she rejected her invitation. She made it clear to Paul that if they were to have a relationship, there would be no pressure from him to make amends with Tamara.

Paul agreed, and asked Selena to come and be with him. She couldn't think of anything better.

The next few weeks were pretty much routine for Selena and Paul. They spent their free time together, getting to know each other even more. They took spontaneous trips to New York, had lunch dates, and he always treated Selena like a queen. She had never felt this good, not even with Sean. Although she knew Sean loved her, they never had the time to experience life together. Sean was devoted to his job as a police officer, and often spent more time at work than with her.

Paul no longer had a career. Selling the nightclubs gave him the freedom to enjoy Selena and all that life had to offer. He invested some money, and even had a few properties on the market, including Selena's house and her salon, which sold last week for $200,000.00. Paul advised Selena to put the money in an account and to just leave it alone. He assured her that she would never have to worry about anything as long as they were together. She didn't plan on going anywhere, and was happy to oblige whatever Paul desired.

She felt free and excited now that she no longer had the salon as an obligation. She had become quite the domestic one, cooking gourmet pancakes and omelettes, and making fresh squeezed juices for Paul every morning. She barely spent any time at her townhome anymore. She enjoyed the huge back yard and serenity at Paul's place. He never complained, so she didn't feel a need to go home.

She had even begun to consider Andrea's offer to take over her mortgage since she spent so much time at Paul's. She initially declined, but had been thinking about it more often. Although her mortgage payment was pennies, and Paul had no problem paying it month after month, it was still an unnecessary expense.

Paul called for Selena while he stood in the steaming hot shower of the master bedroom. It was royal and fully equipped with a Jacuzzi, heated tile floors, and beautiful decor in gold and different shades of brown. The floor length mirrors made the room appear even larger than it already was.

"Yeah, honey?"

"Grab me a towel."

"Please." Selena added in a joking matter.

Paul never responded and held his hand out of the glass shower door awaiting his towel.

"So where you headed, honey?"

Paul stepped out of the shower, his green eyes sparkling

as the water dripped from his awkward body. Selena no longer minded his physique though, he was perfect for her and he knew how to make her body tingle all over. She was becoming horny watching him as he dried his hair with the towel.

"I have some errands to run."

"Oh, well do you want me to come with you?"

"No, stay here. You don't have to go everywhere with me."

He gently kissed her forehead, and proceeded to apply his deodorant and spray his Angel cologne.

Selena was a little annoyed at his statement, but decided to relax and not make a big deal. Maybe he was just having a bad day.

By the time Paul arrived back at his home, Selena had just awakened from a nap. The warm summer air was blowing in the bedroom window, making the peach colored curtains dance with the wind. She lay across the bed, rubbing her pink polished toes up and down the cream satin bedspread. She had fallen asleep naked, after she showered and dabbed on some Viva La Juicy. He walked into the bedroom and smiled at Selena.

"Just the way I like you, baby."

Selena was smiling from ear to ear. Not only because she noticed that he had a gift in hand for his special lady, but because to her, there was nothing better than to wake up and see his face and smell his scent. She gently placed her hands on his face and began to kiss him passionately.

Paul pulled away from the kiss in order to present her with a gift. Selena loved receiving gifts from Paul. He knew what type of gifts would make a woman smile. It was her favorite perfume, Emilio Pucci. Although it was her favorite scent, she was a bit disappointed because he had just gotten her all new perfumes not even a month ago.

She pecked Paul on the lips and began to walk over where she kept her perfume. He grabbed her arm and asked if she was going to open it.

"No, I have a bottle already open. I'm going to just put this one up."

"But I wanted you to see the bottle. It's a limited edition, check it out."

Selena reluctantly opened the box and almost passed out when she lifted the bottle from the box.

Paul had taken a silver satin ribbon and draped it around the bottle, along with what appeared to be a three-carat engagement ring. She was in shock. She realized she was standing there naked and reached for her bathrobe on the bed. When she grabbed it and turned around, Paul was down on one knee.

"Selena, I know it's only been about 7 months since we started seeing each other, but you're all I think about. When I didn't talk to you for those two days, I felt incomplete, and that's when I knew I needed you here with me forever. Will you be my wife, will you marry me?" he stared up at Selena with a tear in his eye, eagerly awaiting her response.

The tears flowed down her cheeks. So many thoughts raced through Selena's head; Sean, Tamara and Arielle, her mother's scent, and even Omar. She was overwhelmed, but knew that she had deep feelings for Paul. She gently touched his face with her hand, lifted his chin, and kissed his soft lips. He could taste the salt from her tears as he wrapped his hands tightly around her waist.

"Don't say no Selena, I love you," he begged.

She held her hand out for him to place the three-carat princess cut rock, which was accented with baguettes around the entire band.

"Yes, yes Paul Major. I will marry you!" she exclaimed.

Paul slid the ring on her finger and watched her admire it while he admired her. Before long, they were wrapped in the satin sheets, making love like they had never made it before.

CHAPTER 10

The next few weeks were hectic. All Selena could dream about was her wedding day. She wanted it huge, glamorous, better than the one that she was planning with Sean. She talked about the wedding every day all day. Paul barely showed interest, and Andrea seemed jealous. She had even called Tamara once to tell her the news and to try to plan another get together. Again, Tamara declined. She had no one to share in her glory. She had everything a woman could ever want, and still felt incomplete.

She mentioned her feelings to Paul, who simply suggested she forget all of this extra wedding planning, and that they simply get married on an island, preferably Hawaii. Selena's hopes of a dream wedding were off again, but she would make the best of her Hawaiian nuptials. All she needed was Paul, anyway.

It was July of 2009 when Selena walked down the sandy aisle that was flooded with purple orchids in Honolulu, Hawaii. She wore a white strapless satin wedding gown. It was simple and elegant with detailed beading that accented the area around her full breasts. The satin clung to her toned physique perfectly. She wore a beautiful lei around her head in various shades of purple. She styled her own hair in a bun that sat neatly atop her head. Her feet were bare and polished in an American manicure, the same as her hands. Her diamond engagement ring sparkled as she walked down the aisle to a sweet sounding harp and native Hawaiian women dressed in colorful pa'u skirts dancing the hula dance.

Paul stood at the end of the aisle in a custom made white linen pant suit. His hair had grown in and was curly all over. He was also barefoot, and had his pants rolled up, exposing his hairy calves. He smiled brightly, showing his beautiful white teeth as his bride floated towards him.

As Selena neared Paul, she began to smell his aroma. He had opted to wear the Prada. That scent normally drove her wild; it was soft, yet masculine, and just a tad spicy. But today, it was giving her a headache. She had finally made it to her groom and felt like she wanted to pass out. She closed her eyes for a moment, took a deep breath, and was able to pull herself together.

Her emotions were at an all-time high, and she had to be strong and get through this moment. This was her new beginning, the next chapter in her happiness.

They stood face-to-face and repeated the words of the official until he pronounced them man and wife. They leaned in to embrace and kiss each other. It was a long, deep, passionate kiss, but Selena pulled away. The smell of Paul's cologne was again bothering her. There were a few claps and cheers from onlookers, and the Majors were on their way. Paul lifted his new bride and ran down the sand until they reached the beautiful blue waters of the ocean.

They kissed and held each other. Selena was soaking wet in her wedding dress and not minding one bit. They headed to their villa to shower and get dressed to prepare for the luau that awaited their arrival.

Selena was excited to be a newlywed, but still felt lonely. She had no one to share her happiness with besides Paul. She even wished she would have at least had Andrea there, who she had originally asked to be her maid of honor when she was planning an actual wedding ceremony. She knew Andrea would be upset when she arrived back home. She and Paul had left without saying a word to anyone. Paul told her that there was no one worthy enough to share in their union. Selena somewhat agreed, and had gone along with Paul's plans to elope.

The food at the luau was delicious– plenty of exotic fruits like pineapple, papaya, mango, different kinds of cheeses, even a kalua pig. Selena was absolutely in love with the bulgogi, which was boneless chicken and rice in a sweet and sour sauce. They sat at the man-made fire pit and fed each other different dishes and talked for hours.

Selena was happy that Paul had showered prior to dinner, and got rid of the Prada that had made her ill at the ceremony. They took another swim in the ocean after the sunset, before they retired to their villa and enjoyed being intimate together the first time as husband and wife.

The next five days flew by. They were so busy partaking in everything imaginable from scuba diving, hiking, and even bungee jumping, they hadn't realized that later on that evening, they would be heading to the airport to travel home.

They sat amongst the piles of clothing that Selena had brought, packing and reminiscing about their weeklong honeymoon. Selena opened up to her husband about feeling lonely that no one was able to witness their marriage. Paul seemed annoyed by Selena's emotional testament and responded to her in a very negative manner that she was not used to from him.

"Well the bottom line is when you reached out to Tamara. If she wanted to be bothered with you, she would have. As far as Andrea, I don't even know why you keep her in your company. Her jealousy and envy towards you are obvious from a mile away. We're all we have, this is our family now. Who was supposed to be here was here." He snapped as he zipped up his luggage bag and stood it upright on the floor.

Selena knew that what Paul was saying was somewhat correct, but she still longed for companionship other than Paul. She was ready to leave the island and get back home and figure out what new hobby she would involve herself in. Since she had sold the salon, she usually stayed at home preparing meals and cleaning or went on shopping sprees. She seriously needed something to do. The newlyweds slept the entire seven-hour flight home to Philadelphia International.

Pulling up in the driveway of their home felt wonderful. Selena had been and still was a homeowner, but now she owned a beautiful million-dollar mansion with her husband, who was handsome and successful. She was on cloud nine, and never wanted to come back down.

She was quickly brought back down when Paul unlocked the front door, and they walked into the foul smelling foyer. Selena gagged, and ran immediately to the guest bathroom down the hall and threw up before she could reach the toilet. Paul rushed to her side and grabbed a hand towel off of the rack to wipe his wife's face. She was sweaty and flushed.

He confirmed that she did not have to vomit again,

then carried her to the family room and laid her across the huge sectional. He ran to the kitchen where he not only grabbed a bottle of water for her, but also found the root of the horrible smell.

"Honey, I found what the stench was. We left that pot of eggs on the stove for the entire week we were gone. You've got to get on the ball with stuff like that, it smells horrible in here."

Selena waited patiently for her water and a sign that Paul was just kidding with his last statement. She received the water, but assumed Paul was serious.

"I've got to get better at it or we've got to get better at it? Because I swore when we left a week ago, we BOTH were excited to get out the door when the car service pulled up. Don't put it all on me."

"At any rate, it smells horrible in here. How are you feeling? I was planning to go out to eat tonight, but you don't seem up to it."

"I don't know what's wrong with me. Everything smells so horrible to me all of a sudden. Even your cologne is killing me."

"I have on Issey Miyake, I thought you liked it. What's been going on with you not liking smells you usually adore, and your huge appetite? Do you think you could be pregnant, baby?"

Paul's face was filled with glee at the thought of pregnancy.

Selena initially brushed off the possibility of pregnancy until she sat and thought about it. She had been so excited and caught up in initially planning a wedding, she couldn't remember if she had gotten her period in June. She knew for sure that she had gotten it in May; it had gone off the week right before the gala. She remembered specifically, because she was hoping it wouldn't be there on the night of.

Paul had begun to take their luggage upstairs, and Selena sat straight up, trying to recall the last month of her life. After almost five minutes of trying to recall, it was clear that she had missed a period in June. It couldn't be true. She couldn't be pregnant. She was a newlywed, ready to travel and try new hobbies. A baby right now would be too much. She needed to know for sure, and CVS was only a five-minute drive away.

When she arrived back home, Paul had gotten rid of the horrid smell, and unpacked their belongings. It was at times like this, she knew that if she were to be pregnant, he would be an excellent father. She nervously went into her master bathroom and followed the directions on the EPT package. Paul sat quietly on the side of their king sized bed, waiting for the outcome.

Three minutes seemed like three hours as Selena watched intensely to see if the red lines would show up on the home pregnancy test. She leaned her head back and ran her fingers through her full shoulder length hair and wrapped it in a loose bun in the back of her head. She opened the bathroom door, and Paul immediately stood up.

"Sooo what's the verdict?"

She held her head down and mumbled the words, "I'm pregnant."

* * * * *

Paul and Selena had just left their first doctor's

appointment where they confirmed the pregnancy and gave her an expected due date of February 2010. She was eight weeks pregnant, and her emotions were all over the place. She couldn't remain happy or sad for more than five minutes at a time. She needed a break from Paul. She needed to talk to someone and have girl talk. She had only talked to Andrea once since she had been back from Hawaii, and she wasn't really happy to hear from Selena since she had eloped with not even a word to the woman whom she had asked to be a part of her wedding.

Paul, of course, had said that it was all out of jealousy, and that Selena should keep her time with Andrea to a minimum, especially since she was now married and pregnant. His theory was that they no longer had anything in common, and a friendship without common ground was a disaster waiting to happen.

Despite her husband's views on Andrea, she had already texted her and made plans to meet up with her later on. Paul had a meeting with an investor, and Selena wasn't about to sit alone in the huge home and wait for him all day.

It was hot and humid the first week of August. They opted to meet downtown because Andrea was off for the day and would already be in town running errands. Selena hadn't curled her hair since she had been back from her honeymoon, due to the humidity. Her sleek ponytail was the perfect look for her long yellow and black sundress from Express and black thong sandals. Andrea was already sitting at a table at Tangerine when Selena walked in, her iPhone in one hand and a Cosmopolitan in the other.

"Heeeeeeyyy stranger!" she yelled out.

She quickly ended her phone conversation and stood up to hug Selena.

Andrea looked adorable in her cut off jean shorts and fitted white and silver Armani exchange tank top. Her hair was just as Selena's was, pulled back in a ponytail, and her lips were perfectly shimmering.

The first topic of discussion was the wedding. Andrea admitted that she was hurt when Selena and Paul decided to elope. It wasn't because of their decision to go away, but because Selena didn't inform her. Selena apologized and quickly began to divulge all the details of their ceremony.

Andrea congratulated her friend and presented her with a gift for her wedding. Selena was shocked. She had started to feed into all of Paul's comments about her and Andrea's friendship, but in the short time they had been sitting in the restaurant, all Selena saw was a true friend.

It was a beautiful crystal picture frame for their wedding picture. It had been engraved with Paul and Selena's name and the year 2009. Selena gave her friend a hug and thanked her. This was the first and only wedding gift that she had received. Before long, Andrea was ordering two more Cosmopolitans.

Selena asked her why she was going to drink two more, this early in the afternoon.

"Chile please, one of them is for you."

"I can't…I mean I don't want to drink right now."

Selena tried to catch herself, but Andrea had already put two and two together.

"Oh my God, you're pregnant."

Selena gave a half-ass smile and nodded in agreement. Andrea was excited and automatically claimed her spot as the unborn child's godmother. Selena sat emotionless.

She was still in shock that she was pregnant, and was neither excited nor upset about the revelation.

Andrea shot questions at Selena like missiles. She asked everything from questions about the baby, to her and Paul, to feelings for Omar. Usually, Selena would be annoyed by Andrea's natural talkative and nosey behavior, but the questions now had her thinking about her life. She sipped her iced tea and began to tackle Andrea's questions.

"I don't know how I feel, Drea. I mean, I am happy to be married to such a wonderful man who adores me, but honestly, I didn't see children in the picture for a while, if at all. It's like I'm just starting a new chapter in life, and I want to enjoy it to the fullest. But at the same time, I know this baby is a blessing and I am going to fall completely in love with her or him the moment we meet. And Omar, please I haven't heard from him since I last saw him in…"

She hesitated as she thought back to when she had last seen Omar, and she began to panic as she realized that she and Omar had been intimate around the time that she conceived. She grabbed her head and forgot she was acting out in front of Andrea, who always knew how to piece things together according to peoples' body language. By the time she gathered herself and looked up, she knew that Andrea had figured out what had gotten her off track.

"Selena, it's okay. I'm here for you. We will figure this out together."

Selena wiped the forming tears with her index fingers and regained her composure before she began to speak.

"Listen Andrea, I'm in a real fucked up situation right now, and you are the only one who knows. I have no one else to confide in but you. The biggest help for me right now would be to keep this between you and me. That's all

I ask of you," she pleaded.

Andrea grabbed Selena's hands across the table. She assured her that her secret was safe with her, and vowed to do anything possible to help her.

For the first time since she had known Andrea, she really felt connected to her; almost similar to the bond that she and her sister once shared. She knew her secret was safe. The two enjoyed lunch, and did not revisit the topic of Selena's pregnancy and the possibility of Omar being the father.

By the end of lunch, Selena felt better than she had prior to it. It felt good to have someone she could trust to confide in other than Paul, and although she still needed to figure out her next move, she now felt confident that it would be her best move.

CHAPTER 11

Selena arrived home at about 6:00 p.m. She was exhausted and wanted to relax. She couldn't wait for Paul to come home so she could cuddle with him. She needed to smell his manly aroma. She was excited to let him know that she had decided to let Andrea rent her home since it hadn't sold yet. She was confident that he would be thrilled not to have that additional mortgage payment to worry about every month.

Selena sat up in their huge bed thinking of her pregnancy and the possibility of Paul not being the father. She decided to call Omar. She needed to get a vibe from him to figure out if it was even worth telling him. She dialed his number and just like it had been doing for the past few weeks, his phone rang and then went to voicemail.

Just as she heard her front door open, her phone rang. It was Omar. She quickly forwarded his call to voicemail and deleted the call from her call history as she went down to greet her husband. She wrapped her arms around his neck, and they began to kiss like they hadn't seen each other in weeks.

The notification alarm on her phone sounded, and while still kissing her husband, she opened the text message behind Paul's head. It was from Omar. She got so nervous that all she could read before she quickly deleted it was, *I MISS U.*

Paul walked into the kitchen and placed his briefcase down on the marble countertop. "You didn't cook?" he asked.

"No, I was out all day as well. Thought you would've grabbed something while you were out. So how did the meeting go?" she asked, helping him take off his suit jacket.

Paul moved away from her trying to help him and responded to her statement. "So you *thought* I would have grabbed something? Why didn't you call and ask me? Wait I know why, you were too busy out gossiping with your friends."

Selena was shocked at Paul's reaction and immediately snapped back.

"First and foremost, I don't gossip. I was out with one *friend* in the singular form, and just like I could have called you, you could have called me." She turned and walked away from Paul.

He became angry and yelled, "Don't walk away from me while we are talking. Typical woman shit, as soon as you start hanging with your friends, you get that whole disrespectful nature. Eye rolling, ghetto ass shit."

"W*hat!*? This conversation is over, because Paul, you haven't seen ghetto yet," she stated as she walked up the steps to their bedroom.

She slammed the door and plopped down on the bed, wondering what had gotten into Paul. Although they had started dating less than a year ago, she had never seen him act in that manner. He was always calm and reserved. She figured things didn't go his way in the meeting. She hoped that he would have a drink and calm down before he decided to come up to the bedroom, because she wasn't in the mood to argue.

She wanted to talk to Omar. She had to delete his last text, and it was all she could think of, especially since Paul had decided to act like an asshole. She decided not to call Omar back tonight, but as soon as the coast was clear tomorrow, she would call him. After all, she could be carrying his child.

CHAPTER 12

O ver the next two months, all Paul could talk about was the pregnancy and all of his business ventures that were going well. Selena had learned that although Paul didn't have a nine to five that he had to dedicate his time to, a lot of his wealth came from previous investments and properties that he brokered. Over the last few weeks, he had closed on a commercial property and made a few hundred thousand dollars from an ongoing investment.

He was a shrewd businessman and even more so as a husband. He was demanding and wanted things to be perfect at all times. Selena didn't mind taking care of her husband, as she didn't need or want for anything financially, but she just wasn't used to waiting on anyone hand and foot. Sean was independent, cooked his own meals, and never demanded anything of Selena. This was something that Selena definitely needed to get used to, and quickly, because she and Paul argued more and more as the pregnancy got further along.

Selena still couldn't believe that she was pregnant and wasn't sure who the father was. This was some Maury Povich type shit that she would normally laugh at, but right now, it was her reality.

She had spoken to Omar a few times since he had

texted her, but had never gotten the nerve to tell him that she was pregnant and that he was possibly the father. She hadn't even told him that she was married. All he knew was that she was in a relationship. It didn't stop him from asking Selena to come and visit. She said she would come, but didn't know how she would pull it off.

Aside from Paul wondering why out of the blue, she needed to go to Miami alone. How would she explain the potbelly she now had as she entered into her sixteenth week of pregnancy, to Omar? This was supposed to be one of the happiest periods in her life, but she was far from happy. She was clueless and miserable.

Homemade lasagna and tossed salad was what Selena had prepared for dinner, it was one of Paul's favorite meals, and she had decided to at least try to keep up with the demands of her husband. She had taken an oath under God, and regardless of the trials and tribulations, she needed to give it her all.

It was almost six o'clock when Paul arrived at home. Selena greeted her husband with a long kiss. He smiled, kissed her forehead, and then leaned down to rub her belly and say hello to the bundle of joy that would be arriving in a few months.

"Something smells delicious."

"It's your favorite, lasagna. Are you ready to eat now?"

"Yes, as long as I can have you for dessert."

He picked Selena up, sat her on the counter, and gently kissed her on the neck.

Selena gently pushed Paul away. Since she's been pregnant, most of Paul's cologne made her stomach turn.

"This one too, baby?" he asked, as he noticed her pushing him away.

Selena nodded as Paul backed up. He told her that he would just go up and shower before dinner, so she wouldn't have to smell it.

As Selena pulled the food out of the oven and made their plates, Paul walked in the kitchen with a pair of red and black checkered pajama pants, and a black tank top. His stomach was getting bigger, and his arms were flabbier than ever. She had heard that some men gain weight when their significant others were pregnant, but Paul didn't need to. His extra weight turned Selena off. He looked more like her uncle than her husband.

They sat at the table and began their meal. Paul asked about the nursery for the baby as they ate. Selena always felt uneasy when talking about the baby because she knew it was a possibility that he wasn't the father, and she didn't have a clue as to how she would pull this off. She knew that children didn't have to look like their parents, but Omar was a dark skinned man, she was fair skinned and Paul was half-white. If the baby was indeed Omar's, she wondered how much of his characteristics the baby would have, and if Paul would ever question the paternity of the child. She thought of every possible scenario, and what fit her needs right now was to never let Paul Major find out.

During dinner, Paul talked non-stop. He had a million and one ideas for the nursery while Selena wanted to wait to find out the sex of the baby before they did anything. They agreed to wait until her next appointment, which was in two weeks. Selena would officially be five months pregnant by then. She would be getting her first ultrasound and they would find out if they were having a boy or girl. Selena wanted to be excited, but considering the circumstances, she couldn't.

Then, Paul broke some news that was music to Selena's ears. He would be going on a weeklong business trip to California. Paul had some friends there and was interested in a business venture that one of them was involved in and wanted to check it out.

Selena played the part of the saddened, lonely wife on the outside, but was full of glee on the inside at the possibility of seeing Omar. She prayed that he had home games during that week, and couldn't wait to book a flight if he did.

Paul ran a warm bubble bath for his expecting wife and massaged her body afterwards with warm oil. They made passionate love for only the second time since Selena found out she was pregnant. Although she wasn't attracted to him, he still knew how to make her feel complete as a woman. They held each other all night and slept in until the afternoon.

Saturday had arrived, and Paul was set to board a flight to California. If all went well, soon he would be the owner of a popular chain restaurant. He would become the CEO of three key locations—two on the west coast, and one in New York City. This would mean that Paul would be away from home more often, which was a plus for Selena. She didn't regret marrying him because she was in love with her lifestyle, but she wasn't sure if she was in love with him. Paul stepping back into the world of business would increase their bank account, and decrease the amount of time they spent together.

He gently rubbed her belly and stood up to kiss Selena's forehead before he headed to his plane.

Before Selena could leave the airport parking lot,

she was on the line with Omar. She felt like she was in high school, laughing and joking with him the entire ride home. She didn't know how she would tell him that he could be the father of her child, but she would figure it out. They agreed that she would fly out Monday and stay until Wednesday before he left for Minnesota.

Selena was excited and felt free. Now that Paul was away, she didn't miss him one bit. There were no demands, no specific meals to cook, and no set time for waking up and "becoming busy" as Paul would say. She was content with eating out, sleeping until noon, and shopping all day, and that was exactly what she was going to do until Monday morning when she headed to Miami.

Selena spoke to Paul briefly before she boarded her flight. She informed him that she was on her way to a spa day and would call him afterward. That at least gave her the three hours that it took to get to Miami. She didn't know how she would handle Paul's calls while in Omar's company, but she knew she would figure something out. Her main objective was to see Omar and let him know about the baby. She was open to any reaction, but she secretly wished he would be happy and want to be with her. Either way, her child would be the child of a millionaire, and that was fine with Selena.

Omar had a car service waiting for Selena at the airport to bring her to lunch at Prime 112. Selena's stomach was in knots the entire ride. Her hands were sweaty, and a few tears dropped on that ride as well. She couldn't believe she was even in this predicament. Tamara would kill her if she knew, and for some strange reason, she wished she did.

She had Andrea to talk to, but she missed Tamara and

Arielle. How could she be giving birth in four months without them with her? She realized she had pulled up in front of the restaurant, and quickly wiped her eyes. She felt weak as she walked in. She asked where the restroom was. She was nervous and needed to gather her thoughts. She was now showing and knew that Omar would notice as soon as he saw her.

She stood in the full-length mirror of the bathroom and looked at her round belly poking out of her green Juicy Couture sweat suit. She pulled her Bijan Black perfume out of her purse and sprayed twice – once on her inner wrists, and once on her neck. It was a rough, yet smooth fragrance; perfect for the windy weather on this chilly October afternoon in Miami. She gently brushed her hair that was parted down the middle and pressed bone straight. It fell just below her shoulders and was back to her natural brownish color. Her face was full, and it actually made her look more feminine than before her pregnancy. She was definitely glowing. She smiled at herself in the mirror and began the journey to the table where Omar sat.

He was in what appeared to be a deep conversation when Selena walked up. He smelled her before he saw her and turned around with a huge smile on his face. The smile didn't necessarily turn into a frown, but more of a look of concern as he noticed her baby bump. He stood and hesitantly kissed her cheek. He ended his phone conversation, and stared at Selena from across the table.

She felt awkward, and decided to break the ice. Before she could do so, Omar glanced down at her finger and noticed the three-carat rock.

"So you took a trip to see me to tell me you're married and pregnant? I'm tryin' to figure you out. You called me and asked to come see me. When I texted you last month and said I missed you, you could have told me then, and I would have left you alone. Where does your husband think you are? I don't have time for no crazy shit with someone's wife."

He turned around and then looked side to side, checking to see if anyone was watching them.

"Listen, Omar, everything happened so fast, and I just needed to come see you."

He quickly cut her off. "Listen, I don't deal with married women, especially not pregnant ones. I have an image to uphold, and this isn't a good look for me right now." He stood up and was about to walk away.

Selena raised her voice, but not loud enough to cause a scene. The last thing she needed was some tabloid posting pictures of her and Omar in their magazine and on the internet. Paul, in general, didn't read them, but he knew a lot of people. All it took was one person to run his mouth.

"I came because this may be your child, Omar."

He turned quickly and sat back down, still peeking over his shoulders and wondering if anyone had heard anything. "What type of games are you playing? You think because you are older than I am, you could run some type of scam on me for money? I'm young, but not stupid."

"This isn't a game."

Selena spoke softly and maintained her cool, even though she wanted to curse him out in the worst kind of way. "The last time we were together was in May. I'm five months pregnant. Now, of course, it's a possibility that my husband is the father, but I'm not sure. I'm not saying the situation is right, I'm just being honest with you. As far as money, he may not be as wealthy as you, but my husband is well off. So it's definitely NOT about money!" she snapped.

"So what's the next move? I got a lot of shit in the works, and I don't need any negative publicity right now. Are you planning to tell your husband or what? We could keep it how it is, honestly."

"You don't even want to know if it's really your child? You are prepared to let another man raise your baby if it's yours? If that's what you want, I'm cool with it. Just stand your ground with your decision."

Selena sat there with a stone face. She was hoping her nonchalant approach worked the opposite on Omar. She wanted him to at least agree to a paternity test.

Omar sat in silence for a while. It made Selena nervous, but she didn't want to lose her "too cool" expression.

He excused himself for a moment and went outside the restaurant. Through the glass, Selena could see him talking on this cell phone. She wasn't sure who he was talking to, but she knew he was talking about their situation. He looked upset and appeared to be yelling; something she had never really seen him do.

Once he returned, he agreed to a have paternity test after Selena had the baby, but he needed her to remain quiet about it. He didn't need anything to be exposed until he knew for sure if the baby was his.

Selena agreed, and was ready to enjoy spending time with Omar for the next two days. Unfortunately, Omar cut that trip short when he told her that he thought it would be best that she head back home after lunch. Selena was shocked and hurt, but still grateful that he was open to the test.

They ate quietly, barely talking. Afterward, Omar hugged

her and said that her arrangements to return were being handled, and by the time she got to the airport, she would be set.

Selena sat on the plane and wondered how she had gotten herself in such a mess. Her head was pounding and she felt nauseous. The woman sitting next to her was wearing an obnoxious fragrance that Selena couldn't put her finger on. It was strong and spicy. Selena could taste the fragrance in her mouth. It was awful, similar to Selena's life. She no longer had a relationship with her sister, and her marriage was not what she had expected. Even if it could be worked out, Selena had complicated the situation even more by being pregnant and unsure of the father.

As she laid her head back, trying to sniff any fresh air that didn't contain the woman's perfume, she felt something she had never felt before; a short swift kick in her belly from her baby. She sat upright, placed her hand on her belly, and felt another kick to her round abdomen. Her face lit up, and a tear dropped from her eye.

* * * * *

Once Paul arrived back in town, things were back to the usual misery. Paul was becoming more demanding, and it was driving Selena crazy. He definitely had control issues, and Selena was over it. Between cooking, cleaning, ironing, and nursery preparation, Selena had no other life. She almost felt like she had to sneak when she wanted to talk to Andrea on the phone, because Paul always had something negative to say. Andrea had become like her sister. She knew everything, but Selena trusted that she would keep her secrets.

The day finally came for them to find out if they were expecting a boy or a girl. Selena didn't mind either way, but Paul was adamant about his baby girl. He always said that he knew Selena was carrying his little princess and couldn't wait to spoil her rotten.

Selena watched in amazement as the doctor ran the sonograph machine up and down her sphere-shaped belly. Paul held her hand as the doctor named each body part and organ as he got to it. The moment they were waiting for had arrived, and the doctor politely asked before blurting it out, if they wanted to know the sex of the baby. They both replied yes. He excitedly spoke the words, "it's a girl."

Paul jumped up, kissed Selena on the forehead, and even gave the doctor a hi-five.

After the appointment at Abington Memorial Hospital, they drove to the place where they had first met, Johnny Manana's, for lunch. They sat across from each other holding hands while they awaited their chicken enchiladas. They would finally be able to finish the nursery, and had decided on the colors pink and gray.

Selena was excited, because regardless of who the father was, she was no doubt the mother. She knew it was just a matter of time before she came up with a master plan. She couldn't wait until Paul excused himself to use the restroom. She quickly pulled out her cell phone and sent the text *It's a girl* to two people: Andrea and Omar. Andrea responded immediately, and was of course excited. Omar didn't respond before Paul returned to their table, so Selena slid her phone back into her olive green Diane Von Furstenberg purse.

The next morning, Selena didn't wake until almost 10 a.m. She felt refreshed, but wondered where Paul had disappeared to. She walked down the steps slowly. She was really starting to feel the weight gain of her pregnancy. As she walked in the kitchen and started to open the refrigerator to pour a glass of orange juice, she noticed that Paul had left a note on the chalkboard menu that read:

NOV.17
SEARCH ONLINE FOR RETAILERS THAT CARRY ITEMS IN THE COLOR SCHEME FOR ZURI, TAKE ALL WHITE SHIRTS TO THE CLEANERS, AND PICK UP ITEMS TO PREPARE CHICKEN ALFREDO FOR DINNER.
LOVE, PAUL

Selena was furious. How dare he leave a to-do list for her, and didn't even have the courtesy to let her know his whereabouts? And who was Zuri? She actually liked the name, but they hadn't even discussed names. This had to end. Mr. Major was about to see a side of Selena he had never seen before.

He answered his phone on the third ring, and before she could even say hello, he started to speak. "I'm in a meeting and will be home at about 6. Is everything ok?"

"No, everything is not ok," snapped Selena. "Who the fuck do you think you are leaving a to-do list? I am your wife, not your fuckin' maid."

Paul quickly cut her off and spoke very quietly. Selena could picture his tight lips pressing against the phone for no one to hear as he spoke.

"This is not the time or place. I will deal with you when I get home."

Selena stood in the middle of her kitchen floor in

disbelief. She shook her head because Paul obviously didn't know who he was dealing with, just like Selena didn't know HIM prior to the marriage. She didn't take orders well and had no plans to begin now. He would be disappointed when he got there because there would be no retailers noted, no shirts taken to the cleaners, and no chicken alfredo sitting on the stove. Hell, Selena wouldn't even be there. She dressed and headed out the door.

She sat in what used to be her living room talking to Andrea for hours. She felt comfortable there since Andrea had all of Selena's furniture in the townhome. She had no use for it when she had moved in with Paul, and Andrea was thrilled to know that she didn't need to buy new furniture to fill up her new rental property.

Selena talked to her friend about Paul's controlling ways and how she just wasn't happy with him. They barely were intimate with each other, and she didn't even find his body appealing anymore. Selena began to cry as she spoke about the hurt that she felt every time she realized that she wasn't sure who the father of her child was.

Andrea consoled her and was ready to help her friend come up with a plan to get through this difficult time. They played the scenarios over and over, debating whether or not Selena should just be honest with Paul and let him know, and each time they came upon that option, they decided against it. Selena knew she didn't want to be with Paul, but he would definitely be a good father to the baby. She figured she may as well stay with him, and if he never asks, she would never tell him that their daughter might be another man's child. Andrea rejected that option, highlighting that Selena would be miserable if she stayed with a man she didn't love. Selena agreed she was half way down Misery Lane, and still had three months of pregnancy to go.

Since Selena had sold the salon, she did have a savings account that she'd never even touched because she had access to all of Paul's finances. She thought of just leaving him and using her own money to start over. That also became a no go. Although the money she had would be enough to afford a new home, she would in no way be able to live the lifestyle she had become accustomed to. Although she had made a mistake, one of these millionaires was her daughter's father, and she would need to be well taken care of.

Selena explained how her feelings for Omar were still strong, and although he was young and immature, she felt if they had the opportunity to give a full-blown relationship a try, it would be perfect. There were only two things that could ruin their chance– Selena's daughter being Paul's and Omar not wanting to give it a try. She knew that unless the baby was his, it wasn't even an option, so she and Andrea came up with the perfect plan.

Since Omar had agreed to a paternity test once the baby arrived, she would get one at that time. If the baby was Paul's, she would stay with him for a while, file for divorce, receive her half of his wealth since there was no pre-nup, and move forward on her own. However, if Omar was the father, the stakes were higher. She wouldn't tell Paul until she filed for divorce, it was finalized, and she had half his money. Then she would leave for Miami and pray that a relationship with Omar would be prosperous. Either option would ensure that Selena and her baby girl would have an abundance of finances and a great opportunity to live a happy life.

It was almost 9:00 p.m., and Selena was on her way home when her phone began to vibrate. It was Paul. She knew he would be pissed that she wasn't home and that his to do list was left undone.

"Where the hell are you at this time of night?"

"I'll be there in about 10 minutes," she stated and hung right up.

When she pulled into the driveway, Paul was standing in the door wearing a pair of sweatpants, and bare-chested. Looking at him standing there with his mid-section hanging made Selena realize how much she did not want to be with him. She prayed that her daughter was Omar's so that when she left this old man, she could be done with him forever. She waddled up to their front door and walked right past Paul without even looking at him.

This infuriated Paul, and he slammed the door so hard Selena looked back to see if the glass had shattered.

"What the hell is wrong with you, Paul?"

"What's wrong with you? Out in the streets this time of night carrying my child?"

Selena rolled her eyes to the top of her head, thinking, *if only he knew.*

"And furthermore," he continued, "my shirts are still hanging in the closet, I don't see any dinner prepared in the kitchen, and I don't remember you asking me to go anywhere."

"*Ask you?* I'm a grown ass woman, and your shirts are still hanging and no dinner is done because I don't take orders well. I didn't sign up for this shit here."

Paul grabbed her by her wrist and stood face-to-face with her. The mixture of his Angel cologne and the rum on his breath wasn't a good mix for Selena. "Let me tell you this. If you weren't pregnant with my child, I would have been slapped your face. You better fall in line and get your shit together. I take good care of you, whatever you want and need are supplied, I expect the same in return." He turned and walked away without even looking back at Selena.

She began to cry and eventually threw up all over the kitchen floor. Paul never came back down to check on his wife, and after she cleaned the foul smelling vomit off the floor, she curled up into a ball on the couch and slept there until the sunlight peeked in the window.

* * * * *

For the next three months, Selena reluctantly dealt with Paul's demanding ways. She no longer trusted his temper, and didn't want to risk him become physical while Zuri was in her belly. She agreed on the name Zuri Noelle. She initially despised the name because Paul didn't ask her for any other suggestions and decided it on his own, but once she did her research, she found out that the name meant "my rock." She knew that once she was born, she would need some kind of strength.

She barely had contact with Omar, but he was still up for the paternity test once she arrived, and that was all that mattered. Everything was in order, and Selena was ready to finally meet her baby girl.

CHAPTER 13

Saturday, February 13, 2010, was an amazing day. Selena had awakened earlier than usual, tipped out of bed where a sleeping, snoring Paul was still knocked out, and began to run a warm shower. Her back was tight, and her belly felt crampy, but she was in a beautiful mood. The smell of her Hawaiian Coconut body wash cleared her nasal passages and freed her mind of any worries, all at once. The warm water ran from her hair to her toes and rinsed the creamy bubbles down the drain.

Selena was intoxicated by the aroma and warm water mix, but sobered quickly when she opened her eyes and noticed the pinkish brown discharge that slid down her leg. She started to panic and yelled for Paul to hurry.

Paul ran into the bathroom, and was in even more shock than Selena. He quickly stopped the water and reached for a towel. He grabbed the phone and dialed the number of Selena's doctor. Within six minutes, the doctor had returned the call and advised the couple to make their way to the hospital. On the way there, Selena began to experience pain, a pain she had never felt before. It was intense and strong, and was appearing every seven minutes. Selena was clearly in labor.

When they arrived at the hospital, Paul helped Selena

undress, and they waited for the doctor to check her cervix. The pain was becoming unbearable, and Paul stood by her side wiping her forehead and feeding her ice chips. This was the Paul she had fallen in love with; the caring, concerned, Paul. It was sad because she didn't get to see that side of him much anymore and really didn't want to. Upon checking her cervix, the doctor informed the Majors that Selena was five centimeters dilated, and in active labor. She declined any pain medications and endured five additional hours of labor until Zuri Noelle entered the world.

Born at 2:07 p.m., weighing seven pounds and eight ounces, she was beautiful. Her face was already chubby, and her head full of a brown colored hair was definitely a trait inherited from Selena. Her hair was straight and resembled a toupee. Her complexion was fair, and her eyes were almond shaped. She was perfect. Paul held her even before Selena did and stroked her head gently and whispered in her ear. The sight of Paul already falling in love with this beautiful baby girl brought Selena to tears with the knowledge that in reality, she may not even be his child.

Once she finally held her precious Zuri, she cried even more and instantly fell in love with everything about her. She held her close and gently sniffed her face. She inhaled a smell like no other. It was sweet, fresh, warm, and unique. She had never smelled any fragrance remotely similar to the smell of her daughter, and it was one that would never be duplicated.

Paul called some colleagues and friends to share the news of his baby girl's birth. Selena opted to text Andrea. She didn't feel like causing a scene at the hospital with

Paul. He didn't care for Andrea, and she didn't care for him. She sent back a happy face and asked Selena to send a picture as soon as she could. Andrea knew she would be able to see her goddaughter soon enough, and wanted this transition to be as smooth as possible. Selena also sent a text to Omar to let him know that the baby was born, but she got no response.

She was too excited about her daughter to even worry about it at the time. At about 5:00 p.m. Paul decided he would go out and get Selena dinner instead of her having to eat the hospital food. Selena opted to take a nap while Zuri was in the nursery.

Selena awakened to the sound of shoes clicking on the hospital floors nearing her room and the strong aroma of none other than Lolita Lempicka perfume. It was Tamara, standing over her, dressed in all black, carrying a bouquet of balloons attached to a teddy bear and a small blue box with a huge pink bow on it. Selena was startled, and wondered how Tamara knew she had given birth, and then it dawned on her that Paul had informed her. She realized that she had probably known everything from the beginning. She and Paul were friends, and in an odd way, she was as happy they were. Even through everything, she was happy her sister was there for the most important event in her life.

"So congratulations are in order, little sis, on the wedding and the birth of the baby." She handed the box to Selena and waited for her to open it.

Selena thanked Tamara for coming to see her, as she opened the gift for Zuri. It was a beautiful charm bracelet with the letters of her name dangling from it. Selena began to cry, and leaned over to hug her sister. They held each other tightly for more than two minutes as they both let the tears roll down their faces. Selena felt secure, and the smell of her perfume, that usually was unbearable, didn't bother her. Selena called down to the nursery, so they could bring Zuri for Tamara to see her.

The moment that Tamara laid eyes on baby Zuri was perfect except for one aspect. Selena longed to see her niece Arielle's face. She was away at college in New York and wouldn't be home until her spring break. Tamara took plenty of pictures to send to her, until she was able to see her in the flesh.

As Selena sat and breastfed her daughter, she noticed that she had received a text message. Tamara passed her the phone, and there it was, a text message from Omar. Selena's face lit up as she read it.

Wow this day came fast. It's All-Star Weekend and I am in Texas. When I return to Florida, I will call you so we can make the arrangements. Congrats.

Selena couldn't expect more from Omar. He didn't know if it was his baby or not. She still felt hurt and out of the blue, felt comfortable enough to begin telling Tamara the details surrounding her marriage and even the fact that she wasn't sure who Zuri's father was. Tamara was supportive and told Selena that she would be there to help her through this time, but that she needed to be sure of what she wanted and how she would handle it.

Before long, Paul was walking into the room with four cheese ravioli from California Pizza Kitchen. Selena was starving and exhausted, and both Tamara and Paul stayed until she ate and then left to allow her some time to rest.

* * * * *

After a short hospital stay, Selena and Zuri were now settled in at home. Zuri was the perfect baby. Selena spent countless hours holding and rocking her and rubbing her nose up and down her soft cheeks. Zuri was turning two weeks old, and this was the first day since she had been home that Paul would be leaving the house, and Selena was relieved. She loved how hands-on Paul was as a father, but she needed some space from him. She wanted to spend time with Zuri alone, and since Paul would be gone for almost a week in Los Angeles, she not only would have mother daughter time, but time enough for Omar to catch a flight to get the paternity test done.

As Zuri napped, Selena helped her husband finish packing for his business trip. She would miss the help with Zuri, but couldn't wait for him to walk out the door. She was beginning to feel overwhelmed. Although Paul was a great father, he still expected Selena to wait on him hand and foot, prepare full course meals, and keep the home spic and span at all times. Whether Zuri was his child or not, Selena was ready for this marriage to be over.

After the last piece of clothing was tucked in his Burberry suitcase, Paul began to kiss Selena, which irritated her. She pulled away, and pointed in the direction of Zuri's room. She walked down the hall with Paul right behind, to peek in her room and see that she was still asleep. Her eyes rolled at the top of her head, knowing she couldn't pull the "Zuri needs me" line.

Before long, she was on her knees in the bedroom performing oral sex on her unappealing husband. She hated being affectionate with Paul, and it seemed like the more she acted uninterested, the more he enjoyed it. She slid her mouth up and down his erect penis faster and harder. She was ready for this to be over with. Shortly after she sped up the process, Paul was moaning and releasing his bleach scented cum in her mouth. Selena had always resented that about Paul. He never once asked if she enjoyed him cumming in her mouth. She knew some women didn't mind, but she definitely did.

Paul was now satisfied. He helped his wife up off her knees, kissed her forehead before he grabbed his suitcase, and headed towards Zuri's room. He gently picked up his baby girl and kissed her cheeks. He walked around in circles in her room, rocking her while she slept. He whispered that he loved her over and over in her ear before he laid her back down and headed for the door.

Paul hadn't even been gone an hour before Selena called Andrea and told her to come over when she got off work. Andrea was excited. She had only seen Zuri once since she was born, and any chance to spend time with her and Selena was fine. Selena ordered a pizza, fed Zuri, and had just enough time to get a shower before Andrea rang the bell. Selena swung the door open and was happy to give her friend a hug and have some adult conversation. She hadn't talked to anyone besides Paul in a week, not even Tamara.

She had been busy trying to obtain some new clients, and promised Selena that she would be over on Sunday to see her and the baby. Besides finding out who Zuri's father was, life was looking good for Selena. Her baby was finally here, she and her sister had reunited, and she could honestly say that she had a good friend in Andrea.

Andrea came bearing gifts. Selena knew she probably

had a bunch of clothes for Zuri and couldn't wait to see them. Zuri was Selena's personal baby doll, and she loved dressing her. It reminded her of when Arielle was a baby. In the bag was exactly what she had expected – an assortment of outfits for Zuri, and a smaller bag that Andrea said was for Selena.

Selena lifted a pink box, adorned with a black rose. It was perfume, one that she had never smelled before. She had never even seen the box before and she was excited to get a whiff. The fragrance was Flowerbomb, and once she sprayed it, she fell in love. It was warm, rich, and full of zest. It had an amazing aroma, and instantly, was noted in her head as her favorite, even above Emilio Pucci.

"Oh my God, that shit smells good. I've never even heard of it before. Thank you so much, Drea, I love it."

"No problem, someone I work with wears it, and it smelled like something that you would wear, so I picked it up for you. I'm glad you like it, now where is my princess?"

"She's upstairs sleeping, and she just went down. *Please* let her sleep. She won't sleep for long, and you can have all the kisses then. She is becoming such a little handful." Selena smiled at the thought of her little angel.

The two chatted for almost an hour, sipping peppermint tea before Zuri woke up. As soon as she heard her squeal, Andrea headed up the steps to grab her. Selena was right behind her and admired Andrea's sweet and sincere interactions with her daughter. She changed her diaper and brushed her hair before lifting her up and kissing her plump cheeks.

"Oh my God, I hope those clothes fit. She is getting so chunky, I love this little girl."

They walked downstairs and Andrea listened and fed Zuri as Selena explained that Omar would be coming to town in two days to take his paternity test. She talked about how nervous she was to actually find out who Zuri's father was. If it was Paul, she at least knew that Zuri would be taken care of, but she would be more likely to stay with Paul because of their child. She prayed it was Omar, so she could divorce Paul, take half his wealth and move away and prove to Omar that with his family was where he should be. Andrea co-signed every aspect of Selena's plan. They both eagerly awaited the next 48 hours.

Chapter 14

It was almost 2:00 p.m., and Andrea hadn't arrived. Selena had already strapped Zuri in her car seat and was ready to leave as Andrea drove up quickly in the driveway.

"Damn girl, you know my appointment is at three. Omar is already on his way there, I was about to leave ya ass."

"I'm sorry girl, traffic is a bitch on the expressway. Let's go, we will make it on time."

Andrea had arranged for the private paternity test through the hospital of the University of Pennsylvania. Since she worked there, she knew a lot of people who worked in the adjacent building. The person who would be performing the test was a good friend of Andrea's, Ji Hong, an Asian female who was the head of the hematology department and also had her own private practice affiliated with the hospital. She agreed to perform the test, and even sign a confidentiality form, as requested by Omar.

The ladies walked into the office at about 2:45 p.m. Selena headed over to the front desk and gave the receptionist her name and was advised to go to Room C and have a seat. She removed the pink Gymboree snowsuit that Zuri was keeping warm in and proceeded to walk to the room.

She looked back at Andrea nervously, but felt better when Andrea winked at her and gave her the thumbs up signal. Selena was shocked to open the door and see Omar sitting at the long conference table with a guest.

They had agreed to keep this between the two of them, at least the actual testing portion. As she walked over to the table, the well-dressed gentleman seated across from Omar jumped up to pull out Selena's chair. Selena opted not to sit in the chair that he had pulled out, and sat right next to Omar, instead. She wanted to know who the stranger was, and she wanted him to look Zuri in her eyes.

"Who the hell is this, Omar? I thought we were going to handle the actual testing alone?" Selena didn't yell, but she still spoke loud enough for the gentleman to hear.

Before Omar could answer, the stranger began to speak. "I'm Everett Carter, Omar's agent, pleased to meet you," he stated with a hint of irritation.

"Agent? Are you serious Omar? This has nothing to do with basketball."

"Actually, Ms. Nichols, it does. Just as we need to sign confidentiality forms for today's procedure, we will also need to sign some for an extended period of time, regardless of the outcome of the test." He smirked at Selena, noticing that she was becoming annoyed.

"Confidentiality regardless of the outcome? What the hell is going on here? Omar you better say something, you are sitting there like you can't speak for yourself, and furthermore, you didn't ask to hold or even see the baby."

Selena was furious.

"Mr. Henderson, I would advise that you wait until the results are in before you start any bonding with the child in question."

Selena looked over at the agent in disbelief, and then turned to Omar and waited for him to speak.

Omar finally broke his silence.

"Everett, chill. Let me talk to Selena without you for a minute."

"Mr. Henderson, I would advise you not to do that…"

Omar quickly snapped at the overzealous agent and advised him in a stern voice to step outside for a moment.

Mr. Carter obeyed Omar's demand, picked up his briefcase, and hurried out of the conference room door, never looking back.

"What type shit is this Omar? What do you mean confidentiality agreement? So you mean to tell me that if this beautiful little girl is yours, you don't want anyone to know? And what the fuck did you bring your agent for? She isn't a basketball, she's a baby, possibly your baby."

Selena's eyes were full of tears by now. She waited for a response from Omar as he stared blankly at Zuri.

"She's beautiful, can I hold her?"

Selena's tears had begun to fall. She swept her long tresses behind her ears, and passed Zuri, who was dressed in a cream Polo dress, cream and pink printed leggings, and the tiniest pair of pink Ugg boots to the other man that could be her father. Selena stared at Omar and Zuri, looking for any resemblance, but there was none. She looked just like Selena. Her complexion, eyes, even her nose was small and button-like just like her mother's. She didn't look like Paul or Omar. Omar rocked her back and forth as he spoke.

"So the confidentiality agreement is an idea my agent came up with because I'm in the middle of contract negotiations, and some major endorsement deals. The next 12 months for me are pivotal, really taking my career to the next level. Don't get me wrong, a baby is a blessing, but with the media and you being married, this could potentially threaten my money. It would only be a 12 month agreement, just enough time for all my upcoming endeavors to be finalized."

Selena sat silently listening to Omar in disbelief. How could any of this mean more than establishing a relation- ship with his daughter? She was on the verge of snapping until she had an epiphany.

If Zuri was Omar's daughter, that year would serve as enough time to execute her plan with Paul, enough time to establish the problems in their marriage, file for divorce, and get her half. She was ecstatic. She tuned back in to hear what Omar was talking about.

"I wouldn't neglect my financial obligation to her if she is mine during that year. We would need to set up an account, to which I would automatically send $15,000.00 a month. We just couldn't spend time together during that time, and you wouldn't be able to tell *anyone* that she is my daughter, or it would breach the contract and stop the funds to the account. I mean, listen, I know it probably sounds crazy to you, but this whole situation is crazy to me. We gotta work together on this."

Omar had pleaded his case, and waited to hear Selena's response as he gently patted Zuri as she lay on his shoulder.

"Alright Omar, I'll sign the agreement. Let's just do it and get the test done so that we will know where we stand with all of this."

Omar walked over to the door and motioned for Mr. Carter to come back in. He sat back down, and explained exactly what Omar had already said to Selena. His demeanor was very snappy. It almost reminded Selena of a female with a bad attitude. Selena was so annoyed with him that she never even complimented him on his magnificent smelling cologne. It had to be, Bvlgari, one of Selena's all-time favorites.

Omar and Selena both signed the agreement, and as soon as the pen touched the table after Selena signed, Mr. Carter had an additional sarcastic comment to make.

"Mr. Henderson, let this be a lesson learned. Every pretty-faced groupie isn't just satisfied with a designer bag or shopping spree, some go for the gusto."

"*Fuck you!* I'm far from a groupie." Selena stood up and began to walk towards Everett just as Ms. Hong walked into the room.

She asked if they were finished with their business, and motioned for Selena, Omar, and Zuri to follow her. The procedure only took a few minutes, and once they were done, Omar and Selena hugged. She held him tightly, wishing that it wasn't under those circumstances. Omar gently pulled away from her and complimented her aroma. She had worn the Flowerbomb that Andrea had bought her.

She thanked him and picked up Zuri and passed her to Omar. He kissed her forehead, and rubbed his hands in the direction of her silky hair, before he handed her back to Selena.

* * * * *

Omar sat in the car with his agent, holding his head. Everett appeared annoyed, but needed to be concerned for his client.

"What's up Omar, what are you stressing about?"

"This whole situation. I am at the peak of my career. She's a married woman. How will it look to just pop up with a kid? Then I gotta deal with the media and her husband. It's just a whole fuckin' headache."

Everett rolled his eyes to the top of his head, but knew his client needed some comforting words.

"That's surely not the worst thing that could happen to your career."

Omar looked up and stared blankly at Everett.

"I mean you could be injured or cut from the team. I'm just saying it's not the end of the world, you'll get through it."

"I guess so, but it sure feels like it. I do thank you for being there for me through everything, and being understanding. You've never turned your back on me, and I appreciate you."

"You know I'm here for you."

"I know, thanks, but right now I am starving. Let's go eat."

* * * * *

Paul seemed to annoy Selena even when he was away. He called almost every hour on the hour, asking the same questions. Her stomach got butterflies every time the phone rang and she saw that it was him. He was a control freak who needed to know everything that was going on at all times. He would be home in two more days, and Selena wished he would take a break from the phone because soon enough, he would be there in the flesh.

She had just laid Zuri down for her nap, and was ready

to get a shower and relax, when her phone rang. She started to ignore it because she assumed it was Paul, but didn't feel like having to explain not hearing the phone ring or making up a lie when he finally did get through. She figured she would just get this call over with so she could have some personal time.

It wasn't Paul on the line, though. It was Ms. Hong. She and Omar had opted to receive the results by telephone, neither one needed mail pertaining to a paternity test coming to their homes. They had set up passwords with Ms. Hong at the office the other day, and before she could read them the results, they had to verify the information, and be conferenced in with the other party.

Once Selena and Omar were both on the line, they spoke to each other and waited to hear what Ms. Hong had to say.

"I won't drag this out for you two. I know the past few days have been hard enough. Selena and Omar, with a 99.99% of accuracy, Omar Henderson, you are the father. If either of you need a written copy of the results, you have my email address. Shoot me an email, and I will get those to you by the method of your choice. Does anyone have any questions?"

They both answered no at the same time.

"Alright then, it's been a pleasure. If you need any further assistance, feel free to contact me, thank you."

The dial tone in her ear brought Selena back to reality. Just like that, her plan was about to be put in motion.

CHAPTER 15

Zuri was growing so fast. Selena couldn't believe that she was now seven months old, sitting up, holding her own bottle, and even crawling. It had been almost four months since Omar was found to be her father, and as the agreement stated, every month on the first, Selena received an automatic deposit of $15,000.00. It was a private account that Paul knew nothing about and that Selena hadn't even spent $10,000.00 out of since she had it.

Paul was a wonderful provider. Zuri had more clothes than she could ever wear, and Selena didn't need for anything, except true love, other than the love she received from her Zuri. Paul was even more demanding. He no longer treated Selena with respect. All of the pampering, and gentlemanly qualities that she fell in love with were long gone. He was, however, a loving father to Zuri. She already had him wrapped around her finger. There were only two problems: Selena did not love him, and Zuri wasn't his child.

* * * * *

It was a beautiful fall day as Selena dressed her little princess. She couldn't believe how much she looked like her. Her hair color, lips, eyes; everything resembled Selena.

She was excited to spend a day with Tamara and Arielle. They had only seen Zuri a handful of times since her birth, and they had a lot of catching up to do. Paul was going golfing with some colleagues, which meant Selena's phone wouldn't be ringing every hour on the hour. He didn't call as much when he was in the company of his friends. The original plans were to meet at Tamara's home, but she called Selena earlier and decided they would meet there.

It was almost noon when they arrived, and Selena ran to the door like a teenager anxious to see her slumber party guests. First to the door was Arielle. Selena wrapped her arms tightly around her niece as they both squealed in excitement. Arielle was taller than Selena, but not quite Tamara's height. Her body had filled out tremendously. She had to at least be a size eight in clothing. Her jeans and fitted Hollister tee shirt fit her snugly. She looked exactly like Tamara did when she was her age.

Looking in her eyes almost made Selena cry. She darted into the house and directly into the bathroom to wash her hands so she could cuddle with Zuri. Tamara moped in the door next. The stench of the Lolita Lempicka caught Selena's nose off guard, but not more than the outfit that Tamara was wearing. Besides the fact that she had her hair in a ponytail, which Tamara always said was only for the beach, she was wearing a pair of white Adidas shell toes, and a pink and white Adidas sweat suit. It was cute, but definitely didn't fit Tamara's style.

"What's up, sis? You coming from the gym?"

"The gym, hell no. Why you ask me that, what you tryin' to say, I'm fat?"

"No, but I don't remember ever seeing you in a sweat suit or sneakers for that matter."

They both laughed.

"Yeah, well I'm relaxing today. I didn't feel like all that today, where's my niece?"

They spent the entire afternoon relaxing, eating, and catching up. Zuri was in love with Arielle and vice versa. At almost 5 p.m., they had worn each other out and lay in a recliner in the den asleep. Selena and Tamara sat in the kitchen nibbling on the last of the Chinese food that they had ordered. Selena thought this was the perfect time to let her sister know about the paternity test and her plans to divorce Paul and move away.

Tamara was shocked and surprised at it all, and sat and stared without a word for a few moments.

"Well little sis, you sure did get yourself in a jam, but I will tell you this, you seem to have come up with a foolproof plan."

Selena felt proud, and although she knew that to most, her situation seemed crazy, there were people who were dealing with situations way more complex. She knew that as long as she kept her mouth shut, and played her cards right, she would end up on top.

Tamara reached into her Givenchy pocketbook and pulled out a picture. It was of an older man, with gray hair, frail and thin, sitting on Tamara's couch at her home. Selena knew in an instant, it was Tamara's father Carl.

Selena glanced at the picture and quickly handed it back to Tamara. She still wasn't comfortable talking about the situation, because she had so many unanswered questions and mixed emotions. She treasured the fact that she and Tamara were together again and didn't want ill feelings or the past to interrupt the harmony.

"I only wanted you to see him because he did mean

something to me. I know he wasn't your father, but he was a good man. I wish you would have met him before he passed, Selena."

Tears raced down her cheeks.

"Had I known the truth about it all before he came home from prison, maybe just maybe, T, I would have been open to it. But why don't you understand how I feel about it? You know who you are, I can't say the same."

"You are Selena Nichols-Major. What do you mean? I never complained about taking care of you, being a mother and father to you, yes we had Grandma, but I raised you. Why can't you see it as me guarding you against the hurt of our life story?"

"T, this isn't what I wanted today. I don't want to talk about all of this shit from the past. It's a new beginning. Look at our daughters in there; we need to get over all this old shit." She raised her voice a bit.

Tamara noticed that Zuri had slid down off of Arielle and was making her way into the kitchen, crawling around in her yellow onesie. Zuri waking was the cue for Selena and Tamara to end the conversation. They both gathered their thoughts and focused their attention on the angel who had just crawled into the kitchen.

Tamara reached her hands out to pick up her niece, and she started to scream. Selena picked her up and rubbed her back gently until she settled down. She watched Tamara's every move for the remainder of their visit, and only went to Selena or Arielle.

"Stranger anxiety in babies is the funniest thing. You'll be fine soon, mama. Before long, you'll be calling Auntie to come rescue you from your crazy mammie."

Tamara and Selena burst into laughter.

CHAPTER 16

It was a week before Zuri's first birthday party, and Selena was running around like crazy making sure she had everything she needed for her princess themed party. Selena and Andrea had just left Bella Baby boutique, picking up the perfect pink party dress for Zuri, when her cell phone rang. She thought for sure it was Paul, being his regular annoying self, but she was wrong. It was Tamara.

"Hey, T, what's goin' on?"

"Hey, where are you? Did you forget about me?"

"Oh shit, I sure did forget. I'm out with Andrea getting some things for the party Saturday, but it's only 4 p.m. You wanna get together at like six or so?"

"No it's ok. Go ahead finish doing what you have to do. We'll get together. Maybe after the birthday party, we will make plans. You've been running crazy, and it's the second time this week you forgot we were supposed to have lunch, so let's just wait until afterwards."

"Ok sis, sounds cool. I will call you later."

She hung up and continued with her conversation with Andrea.

It was almost 8 o'clock when Selena arrived at home, and she was exhausted. Her plans were to give her baby girl a kiss, take a hot shower, spray her body with a fresh fragrance, and fall off to sleep. Those plans literally slapped her across the face before she could even close the front door of their home.

Selena screamed, initially thinking that a burglar was in her home. When she turned her face back towards where the slap came from, she saw a red faced Paul standing there enraged.

"What part of being a wife don't you understand? I have been calling you for over an hour. Something could have been wrong with your daughter, and you're out in the streets like some whore!" Paul yelled.

Selena knew she couldn't beat a man, but she had never been hit by a man before in her life, and wasn't going to settle for it. Her small fist jumped up and punched Paul in his nose. He grabbed her by her shoulders and pushed her against the front door. Selena struggled and tried to pull away from Paul's grip, but she couldn't.

He held her against the door, tightly gripping her pale arms, taunting her, and calling her degrading names. It wasn't until he heard Zuri's cry that he let her go. The tears chased each other down Selena's face. She walked slowly into the bathroom where she stood silently in the mirror. She pulled her long tresses back into a ponytail and rinsed her face with cold water before she headed into the kitchen.

As Paul made his way down the stairs with Zuri, Selena was in the kitchen making a bottle.

"There is your beautiful mommy," Paul said in an innocent, sweet tone.

Selena knew at that moment that something was wrong with Paul, and she wanted out. She thought of leaving once he fell asleep, but knew that he would hear her gathering

Zuri's things. Although she knew he would never hurt her, she wasn't about to leave without her daughter.

She needed to talk to someone, and the only two people she trusted were Tamara and Andrea. Paul had a meeting the next morning, and she needed to talk to them. She needed help, and she needed it fast. After she fed Zuri, she slid into her bed. She lay dangerously close to the edge, not wanting to be able to feel the heat from Paul's flabby body. Their bed was cold and unscented, reminiscent of their marriage.

Selena was awakened by the smell of Paul's cologne. Ever since she was pregnant with Zuri, it was Angel, but nowadays, it was more like Devil. It was strong, arrogant, and demanding, just as Paul was.

Selena was sore and felt weak. She glanced over and saw that Zuri was lying on Paul's side of the bed, enjoying her bottle. She leaned over and kissed her forehead before she attempted to get out of the bed. Her arms felt heavy, and were adorned with purple bruises, from Paul's tight grip. Once she entered the bathroom and looked up, her blood began to boil. The entire left side of her face was purple from the open hand slap to the face administered by Paul.

She was enraged and wanted revenge. She turned around and stormed out of the bathroom, only to realize that they weren't alone. This was no longer about Selena and Paul, Zuri was laying on the bed resting peacefully as Paul stroked her hair gently. Selena held in all emotions—the anger, sorrow, hurt, and disbelief. She inhaled deeply to keep one single tear from falling and was able to smell the aroma of her Flowerbomb perfume that saturated the sweater she left draped over the bathroom door. She fingered her hair back into a ponytail, returned to the bathroom and started the shower.

* * * * *

By noon, Tamara had arrived at her sister's home. She didn't know what was wrong. All she knew was that she had received a text stating: *please come by today, as early as possible. I need to talk to you.*

Selena had never gotten dressed after her shower. She lotioned her body, put on a nightgown and threw her purple terrycloth robe on top of it. Tamara was surprised to see her sister still in pajamas when she arrived, and was even more surprised to see that she had a huge bruise on her face.

"What the hell happened to your face?"

"Paul is what happened to my face, and I don't play this shit. We ain't never been those females to be getting beat on, and it's not gonna start now. Me and Zuri gotta get outta here. I need to file for divorce like yesterday. This man is crazy, and I am not subjecting my daughter to this bullshit, especially since he's not even her father."

"I can't believe he did this. I would have never guessed that this type of behavior was a part of his character. You do need to get away, but divorces take time, especially when there is money involved. About how much is Paul worth these days?"

Just before Selena could give the figure, the doorbell rang.

"Are you expecting someone?" Tamara asked, looking around in concern.

Selena sat her cup of tea on the countertop and informed

her sister that she was expecting someone before she walked towards the foyer to answer the door.

Tamara stood in the kitchen trying to make out the voice of the person at the door, but couldn't quite put her finger on it. Before long, Selena walked back in the kitchen with Andrea close behind her. Tamara rolled her eyes to the top of her head when she saw who it was and barely spoke as Andrea greeted her with a grand hello. Andrea didn't seem bothered by Tamara's lack of manners, but Selena noticed it and made a questioning gesture at her sister, trying to find out what her problem was.

"So T, last I checked, he was estimated at about —"

Tamara cut her off. "Selena, we can talk about it later." She motioned towards Andrea, who had her back turned, grabbing the iced tea out of the refrigerator.

Selena flagged her sister and continued speaking. She stated that Paul was worth at least $12 million dollars, and she wanted half.

"I know that's right, girlfriend. Look at your face, did you call the police on his ass?" Andrea questioned.

"I didn't, because everything becomes public record. A domestic violence arrest could possibly screw up some pending business ventures he has, and that's money out of my pocket."

She hi-fived Andrea and reached her hand out for Tamara, but she ignored the gesture.

"If you file a report, you would probably be granted the divorce earlier and easier." Tamara informed her. "On what grounds will you be filing for the divorce?"

"I know T, but trust me, I got this. I'm still filing under the grounds of abuse. I will just tell them I was scared to go to the police because of what he said he would do. The good old battered wife line," she chuckled. "But I do want to get in contact with a lawyer as soon as possible, so that someone is a witness to the bruises." Selena added.

"I may have a few suggestions for a divorce lawyer, but I will have to call you with the info when I get home. I don't have it on me." Tamara said as she began to reach for her pocketbook.

"You leaving, T? I thought you wanted me to curl your hair, it looks like it broke off."

"Let's just say you aren't the only one under a lot of stress, and yeah, I'm leaving. I have a few runs to make. Just make sure you are careful with your business, Selena. You've been doing a lot of things against the code lately," Tamara snapped.

Selena looked over at Andrea because she knew what Tamara was referring to, and she felt embarrassed for her. She followed her sister, who appeared to have lost at least twenty pounds over the past year, to the door. Tamara had always been curvy and "thick" in her own words. She appeared to be almost about a size 8, now. She hugged and kissed Tamara, then Selena whispered for her to call her later as they hugged at the door of Selena's home.

When Selena returned to the kitchen, she quickly apologized on behalf of her sister. She had become very fond of Andrea and didn't want Tamara's words to hurt her feelings, but at the same time, thoughts of Andrea betraying her began to run through her mind. She wondered if breaking the "Code" that she and Tamara lived by, of only confiding in each other would come back to bite her in the ass. It was too late now. Andrea knew everything, and only time would tell if she would remain loyal. Selena's daydreaming was cut short when she heard Zuri's high-pitched cry blaring through the baby monitor.

Later that afternoon, Selena received a text message from Tamara with an email address for a divorce attorney named N. Angela Owens. She was excited. She couldn't wait to finish making the stuffed flounder and fresh broccoli that Paul had called and requested earlier, so that she could email the lawyer and get the process started.

Initially, Selena had thought not to cook, clean, or do anything around the house. She was disgusted that Paul had put his hands on her, and not even so much as apologized, but she didn't want any additional friction. She would accommodate his demands, because she knew that it was only a matter of time before she would be on her way to build a life in Miami with Zuri's real father, Omar.

Paul didn't come in until after 9:00 p.m., and it didn't bother Selena one bit. She had enough time alone to eat her dinner, spend time with Zuri before she put her down for bed, and email Ms. Owens about the divorce. The day had gone almost perfectly until after Paul ate and showered. He climbed in the bed, and started caressing Selena, wanting to be intimate.

He made her stomach spin. She had no longer had any desire for him, especially since he had put his hands on her. All she could think about was the divorce and the money. She closed her eyes and lay still while Paul inserted himself into her barely moist womanhood and pounded her for almost twenty minutes until he reached his climax. She felt horrible afterwards, turned her back to Paul, and held her pillow tightly until she fell asleep.

It was almost 2:00 p.m., before Selena got a response email from Ms. Owens. With Paul in his office on a conference call, and Zuri napping, she knew she had enough time to read her response and find out what the next step would be. Her response was very detailed. She explained her fees, the process, and what information she would need from Selena. It also stated that she would be happy to assist her.

Selena was excited. She responded, stating that she was ready to begin, and that she would have no problem with handling the fees. Ms. Owens responded back quickly with a time and date for their face-to-face meeting to get everything underway. February 15, 2010 couldn't come fast enough for Selena. She immediately texted the information about the lawyer to Andrea, who sent back a smiley face, and told Selena to kiss the baby for her. She added that she would see them on Sunday at Zuri's birthday party.

At midnight on February 13, 2010, not only did Zuri turn 1 year old, but snowflakes began to fall and continued to coat the ground. By morning, 8 inches of snow had made it impossible for Zuri's birthday party to go on. Selena was annoyed at Mother Nature, but was still excited that her precious daughter had turned one year old.

She decided to dress Zuri up in her pink party dress despite not having any guests. She wore her tiara and danced and played through the house. Paul bundled Zuri in her cream-colored snowsuit and carried her outside to play in the snow while he shoveled the driveway. Selena watched them play from the window and admired how much Paul adored Zuri, but she still had bruises on her arms and her face, and would never be able to forgive him.

Selena's phone had been ringing all morning from Andrea and Tamara to Arielle, all calling to wish Zuri a happy birthday. They all vowed to get there as soon as the roads cleared, which would be at least another day or two. The sound of her T-Mobile jingle broke her from the deep thought she was in while staring out the window. She walked swiftly to the kitchen where her phone was sitting on the table. She hesitated at first, but decided to answer the phone. After all, Omar was her father.

"Hello," she answered in a soft whisper, running back to the window to assure that Paul was still shoveling.

"Hey, how are you? I was trying to wish Zuri a happy birthday."

Selena knew that she couldn't give Zuri the phone, so she lied. "Aww, how sweet, I didn't think you remembered. She's napping right now, but I can have her call you back when she awakes."

Selena held on tightly to the tears that had swelled up in her eyelids.

"That would be nice. So how are you, how is the married life treating you?"

"It's definitely a task to keep a relationship together, and I will leave it at that. How is work?"

Selena didn't want to talk about Paul. She still didn't believe that he had put his hands on her and didn't so much as even apologize.

"It's going well, next weekend is All-Star Weekend in L.A., so I'm looking forward to that. But uh... I just wanted to call and wish Zuri a happy birthday. It's been a while since you've sent me any pictures of her. It would be nice if you could."

"Ok yeah, I need to go check on her, but I will send you some new pictures of her, she's beautiful. Take care Omar, it was good to hear from you."

Selena quickly hung up before Omar could respond,

because Paul and Zuri were on the way in.

"Hey princess, did you have fun in the snow?"

Selena removed the snow-covered outerwear from her daughter and put on her pink and purple Dora the Explorer pajamas. They wrapped up in a blanket and cuddled until they were both asleep.

CHAPTER 17

The day had finally arrived. Selena would officially be filing for divorce from Paul. Luckily, Andrea was off and could keep Zuri while she went to meet with Ms. Owens at her office. Selena was excited as she parked in a lot a block away from the Market Street office. Once inside, Selena boarded the elevator to the fifth floor of the beautifully architectured building. Her pin curls bounced as she walked down the long foyer in search of Suite 526.

She opened the door and was immediately greeted by a young, energetic receptionist. She informed her that she was there to meet with Ms. Owens and was directed to have a seat. She waited almost ten minutes until the receptionist finally summoned her. She walked down a hallway until they reached the third door. The name, N. ANGELA OWENS ESQ hung on the door in gold lettering.

When the door opened, Selena immediately smelled the aroma of a strong, raspy scent that she did not like, Chanel N°5. She walked in slowly, trying not to focus on the fragrance, but it was overwhelming. She couldn't understand what woman would want to wear something so loud.

She admired the artwork in Ms. Owens' office. On

the walls hung paintings and portraits of strong women, from Rosa Parks to Oprah Winfrey. Selena sat down in one of the chairs that were directly in front of the desk, and continued to wait. She admired a picture of a little girl that sat on her desk. She was adorable. Selena smiled brightly and thought of her Zuri, which prompted her to text Andrea to see if she was all right.

Before she could finish the text, a side door adjacent to the office opened and when it did, another blast of Chanel N°5 and a very familiar face emerged. Selena was shocked. She glanced back at the picture on the desk and knew for sure by the complexion and eyes, that it was Sean's daughter, and the attorney was Nadiyah Angela Owens, Sean's mistress. She walked over to her desk, dressed in a fitted black pantsuit and a pair of black and white pumps, and held her hand out for Selena to shake.

"You have got to be kidding me. I'm sorry, this is a conflict of interest. I'm sorry I won't be needing your services."

Selena grabbed her pocketbook and jacket, stood up, and proceeded to leave the office.

"Mrs. Major, you may just want to have a seat and hear me out. I would have no problem representing you, business is business, you can trust me. I would never tell a soul that your husband wasn't the father of your child, that you are receiving a monthly income from her real father, or that you are plotting to receive half of your husband's worth and leave him without letting him know that the baby isn't his."

She smirked and sat at her desk. She began typing as if she had not a care in the world.

Selena stood motionless. She couldn't believe that the

woman who had conceived a child with her deceased fiancé was now a lawyer and knew her deepest secret. Thoughts ran through her head, as she wondered who could have told her. She knew instantly who had betrayed her. It had to be Andrea.

"Listen Nadiyah, please don't believe everything that you hear. Like I said, this is a conflict of interest, and I will be leaving now," she snapped.

"That's fine Mrs. Major. All I know is whether its fact or fiction, all it takes is for someone to mention and even get a doubt in your husband's head about the paternity of your daughter. Once the divorce proceedings begin, they will ask for a DNA test. Your husband is a wealthy man with an estimated worth of almost $15 million dollars. When wealthy men have doubts about anything, they get to the bottom of it."

She continued typing on her computer, not even once looking up at Selena.

Selena turned around and looked desperately at Nadiyah. "So what do you want from me, what is it?" she asked as she plopped down in the seat facing Ms. Owens.

She fought back tears as she looked at a beautiful little girl on the picture who looked just like Sean.

Nadiyah then explained that she would still represent Selena and be able to get her a substantial amount of money from Paul. She also told her that once she agreed to hire her as her attorney, she would be legally obligated to sign a confidentiality form and would not be able to disclose any personal information about her client. It eased Selena's mind to know that by law, Nadiyah couldn't speak a word about her situation. Once they went over the legalities, Nadiyah presented her with another form.

It was her purpose for wanting to represent Selena, and it was blackmail at its finest. She wanted Selena to pay her monthly out of the funds that were sent to her from Omar.

She demanded $10,000.00 a month during the divorce proceedings, and once it was final, she wanted a whopping $1,000,000.00. Selena sat in awe and thought deeply about what was happening. She knew that once the divorce was final, she would still need to remain silent because she was under agreement with Omar. Andrea had set Selena up and was most likely going to be receiving some of the money as well.

Selena's hands were tied behind her back. She was in a lose/lose situation and couldn't afford for her secrets to be exposed. The biggest issue at hand was finalizing the divorce, so she agreed to Nadiyah's terms. She hurried out of the Chanel stenched office, rushing to get to Andrea. She couldn't believe that someone she had grown fond of, had stabbed her in the back. She was enraged.

Andrea opened the door of the townhome she was renting from Selena, not knowing that a tornado of a woman named Selena was on a warpath.

"Where is my damn daughter? Get my daughter's things together and let me get the fuck out of here before I hurt you. You are a fuckin' snake!" she hollered.

"What is wrong with you? You need to calm down, because not only is Zuri sleeping, but I do pay the bills in this muthafucka, and you ain't about to be hollerin' like that up in here."

She slammed the front door that Selena had left open.

Selena was shocked, and in an odd way impressed that Andrea had stood up for herself. In all the years that they had known each other, she tended to play the puppet to

Selena's aggressive behavior.

"Oh, so Andrea has heart now? That's new, only thing you've ever had was a big ass mouth, gossiping all over Philly, telling people my fuckin' business. So how much Nadiyah got for you? I know your ass is getting a cut, pitiful ass, plotting on a so-called friend so you can live my life. One thing about Paul, he was right about your snake ass."

"I don't know what the fuck you are talking about, but like I said, you are not going to keep disrespecting me. So let me gather up the baby's belongings and you can go, you are definitely on some other shit tonight."

Andrea turned and began to walk away.

"And remember, this is my house, and you are now on a month to month lease. Come tomorrow, you will be receiving your official 30 day notice to vacate the premises."

"Something is definitely the fuck wrong with you. But you know what? Do what you have to do. I will be ok, whether I'm here or not."

She handed over Zuri's Juicy Couture diaper bag and then passed her to Selena. The door quickly slammed as soon as Selena stepped down from the step.

Selena couldn't wait to get home. This had been the day from hell. So much was on the line, and her stomach was in knots. She didn't know who to trust or who to believe. She knew at any given moment, Paul could be notified that Zuri was not his child, and if he found out before their divorce was final, she would lose out on the money. She was still under a contract for another year to remain silent about Omar being her daughter's father. Now that Nadiyah had tapped into that money, there was no way she would be able to live off the amount that would be left if Paul found out.

She had to remain calm for the next few months. She was walking on eggshells, and she didn't like the feeling. She felt relieved to pull up in the driveway and not see Paul's car. She needed some time alone once she settled Zuri in. She had to gather her thoughts and relax. She turned the key to her front door and walked into the foyer where she tossed her keys on the table.

Her eyes widened when she walked in and smelled that fragrance that had annoyed her since Tamara started wearing it, Lolita Lempicka.

"Tamara?" She called out, wondering if she was there, and if she was, how she got in.

She quickly removed Zuri's coat, laid her down in her playpen, and began to walk back to the kitchen.

She screamed as she noticed Tamara sitting in the kitchen drinking a glass of red wine. "Why didn't you say anything when I called you? And how did you get in? And what do you have on?"

Tamara sat with her hair pulled back in a ponytail, no makeup on, and an ill fitted sweatsuit. Fashion and style had always been her forte, but lately, she had been slipping.

"Well hello to you too, and to answer your questions, I caught a cab here. Paul let me in before he left. He said you would be home soon, and that he didn't mind if I waited for you. I hope it's not a problem."

"No it's not, I've just had one crazy ass day. You won't believe what the fuck happened to me."

She grabbed the bottle of wine and poured some before she took a big gulp.

"So, first off, you know I met with N. Angela Owens, the lawyer that you recommended to me. You wouldn't believe who it turned out to be—"

Tamara interrupted her before she could finish.

"Well, my day wasn't too great either. Actually Selena, my life isn't great right now. Since my father died, my business folded, and I lost my house. I've been real fucked up, but you didn't know that because everything has been about you and your twisted little soap opera of a life that you have going on. Every time I've tried to talk to you about what's going on in my life, you've never been interested, never took the time to even listen to me. I will admit, neither one of us are perfect, and I totally understand how you could be hurt about me not telling you the truth about my father, but this is how I was raised— to protect you and to keep you from being hurt. In the end, you were still hurt, and now we're both hurt.

"My whole life has revolved around a lie and protecting you, and when shit got fucked up for me, I didn't have anyone there to protect me. Once we began speaking again, I thought things would go back to normal, and I would have my best friend and confidante, but I didn't. You turned even more selfish than ever, consumed with your own life and busy building friendships with other people. I caught a cab here because I don't have a car. I now live in an apartment in West Philly, and I'm living off of savings that are dwindling down fast because I have a child in college whose other parent has decided to not help me financially. Of all people, I thought I could count on my sister for some help, but I haven't even been able to get so much as a conversation from you after all you have put me through. How about the time you took my daughter to get an abortion without letting me know, and she almost fuckin' died, huh? Do you remember that?"

Tamara was now in tears, and Selena stood quiet, listening to her sister's rant. She had heard enough. As much as she loved Tamara, she was already going through enough in her life. She couldn't believe she was piling on all her problems and acting as if Selena was the cause.

"I mean, I apologize if you felt like I should have been there a little more, but I have my own issues, and yes, I do still feel some kind of way about the entire Carl situation. So excuse me if I haven't listened to your problems, and like I was trying to tell you about Nadiyah, I'm now being blackmailed by this tramp thanks to Andrea running her mouth and letting her know my business. I have some real shit going on as well." She snapped sarcastically.

Tamara started to laugh very loudly, and Selena quickly told her to keep quiet because Zuri was sleeping. She asked her what had gotten into her, while snatching the wine bottle that Tamara was reaching for. She assumed that she had too much to drink, which is why she was acting out of character.

"This was too easy, Selena. I thought I taught you better."

Selena slammed her flute down on the countertop and demanded Tamara tell her what was going on. She felt nauseous. Tamara's perfume was really getting to her. She walked over to the sliding glass door attached to the kitchen and flung it open, appreciating the fresh air that flew in.

"What's going on is you are about to help get me back on my feet, and you didn't even know it. Don't worry little sis, your secrets are safe with me because if we don't pull this off, I won't get my money when the divorce is final."

She smiled at Selena.

It finally dawned on Selena. Tamara, her own sister had set her up. It wasn't Andrea, after all. Selena was enraged, and immediately charged at Tamara, causing her to fall off the stool that she was perched on. Tamara was able to push Selena halfway across the room. She had to weigh at least 70 pounds more than her, and had her in height by 3 inches.

"If I were you, I would calm ya ass down. I haven't signed any agreements to keep my mouth shut about anything. It would be great to get that $500,000.00 once your divorce is final, but if you act crazy, I will blow ya fuckin' cover and keep living how I am now. You're the weak one. I'm the survivor. Everything has been handed to you from money, opportunities, love, everything. I've always had to work extra hard for mine, but see, it's easy now, I'm making money off of your fuck-ups."

She picked up the bottle of wine and proceeded to drink out of it. Selena was in shock. This was not the Tamara she knew, and she wasn't interested in getting to know her either.

"What's the matter, little sis? You look confused. This was destined to happen. We are our mother's children. You obviously got her slutty behavior patterns, and I inherited the snake-like qualities. Kind of crazy how it didn't come out til our thirties, huh? I mean, just think, they've always been there for both of us. Come on, you didn't pay attention to how many people I had to shiest to get my business started? I think the problem is that you never paid attention to your behaviors. You portrayed yourself to be Miss Perfect, but what about Sean's friend from the force that you fucked? Or Lorenzo in Jamaica, huh, sis? You should have paid close attention to me, not Andrea. Remember, I *know* you like no one knows you. I raised you."

Before Selena could respond, she heard the small voice of Zuri crying from the family room. Zuri was the only thing that truly belonged to her and that she truly loved. She ran to pick her up. She was soaking wet, and before Selena went up to change her, she advised Tamara to leave. Tamara obliged, but before she left, she tried to reach out to touch Zuri.

Selena quickly laid her head down on her shoulder and turned away. "You will never see her again. Get out now."

Selena didn't even have time to absorb what had just happened because right after she changed Zuri, Paul was walking in the door. She had to get back to her schedule, which consisted of making sure Paul was fed and having sex with him every night. She couldn't wait for this nightmare to be over.

CHAPTER 18

One week after Selena realized she had been set up, and that she needed to be careful until the divorce was final, Paul was served with his divorce papers. It was a Tuesday evening and Selena had prepared a wonderful beef pot roast, homemade mashed potatoes, and fresh spinach. The aroma in the house was edible, but the entire mood of the home changed when Paul walked through the front door and slammed it.

He yelled out Selena's name as loud and strong as he could. He was so loud that it startled Zuri who was playing on the kitchen floor. Selena stood at the kitchen sink for a moment. She closed her eyes and gathered her thoughts before she reached down to pick her up. She knew exactly what he was upset about, and was ready to deal with his reaction.

He stood in the doorway, briefcase in hand, tie hanging from his collar. His face was beet red and Selena could smell the alcohol on his breath. It was overpowering the Angel that he had sprayed on that morning before he left. He dropped the briefcase and walked slowly toward Selena who stepped back with every step forward he took.

Zuri was in her arms, and after the third step backwards, she sat her down on the floor where some of her toys were.

"So this is what you wanna do?" he yelled as he pulled the folded papers out of his suit jacket.

"You wanna up and leave, take my daughter away from me, after all I have done? Provided a beautiful home, made it possible for you to not have to work, and you wanna leave?"

He was finally in arm's reach of Selena. He slapped her face and walked past her like she was road kill as he walked into the kitchen and poured himself a glass of wine.

Selena grabbed her face in disbelief and jumped quickly to her feet. She wasn't about to let this man continue to beat up on her. She had never been a victim of domestic violence, and wasn't going to accept it now. She picked up Zuri while he yelled and screamed. She placed Zuri in her playpen where she was safe, and made sure she had some things to play with. Selena then made her way into the kitchen to wait for whatever Paul was going to do.

He walked back towards Selena, yelling all types of obscenities. Selena was nervous, her armpits were sweaty, and her legs were trembling. Just as he reached out to grab her again, she picked up the bottle of Charles Shaw Merlot that he had just opened and swung it fiercely. The sweet red wine splattered all over their flawless kitchen, and Paul's forehead began to leak in a color almost identical to the wine.

He lifted his right hand and wiped in the area of the blow, realized it was bleeding and dove towards Selena. "You stupid bitch, I should have never married you." he yelled as he pinned her down on the kitchen floor and started choking her.

At first, Selena kicked violently, full of energy. But as

his grip tightened, she lost strength. She began to see stars, and began to throw up. When she started to choke on her vomit, Paul jumped up. He was upset that some of the vomit got on his shirt, and he turned around and spit on her face as she lay there gasping for air. Paul walked away and up the stairs.

As she lay there, she heard him start the water to take a shower. Her first thought was to pick up the biggest knife she could find and attack him while he showered. Instead, she decided to call the police and have something to hang over his head in case her secret was revealed to him before the divorce was final.

Selena limped over to the phone and dialed 911. She whispered the address, and that she needed help, being careful to make sure that Paul didn't hear her. She knew it would blow his mind to know that she had called the authorities. He was arrogant in that manner, and thought he was untouchable and that his money made it ok for him to treat Selena cruelly.

Within five minutes, the police were knocking at the door. Selena quickly ran with tears in her eyes to the safety of the officers. Paul had just gotten out of the shower. He ran down the stairs with a towel wrapped around his waist, his unsightly man boobs shaking with each step he hit.

"Can I help you officer?" he asked as if he and Selena weren't just fighting.

Selena immediately began to scream and tell her side of the story, still covered in vomit, cuts on her hand from the broken wine bottle, strangle marks on her neck, and a busted lip from the first initial slap.

The officers directed Selena to calm down so they could hear her, and Paul walked closer to the door where they stood.

The taller, deep voiced officer directed Paul to step back and relax. Initially, Paul was disobedient, but when the officer stood eye to eye with Paul and warned him that if he didn't keep quiet, he would be arrested, Paul obliged.

After listening to each of their stories, the officers arrested Paul. He began to yell, and even tried to resist arrest before he was finally subdued and placed in a squad car.

Selena gathered their belongings and bundled up Zuri, who didn't so much as make a sound through it all. She hopped in her truck and traveled to the station to file charges against Paul.

He remained in a holding cell overnight and was formally charged with Assault and Reckless Endangerment. He was able to post bail, but was given a stay away order, meaning he wasn't able to go to the house, and had to stay away from Selena and Zuri until their court hearing. He did contact Selena via telephone, at first threatening her, but then changed his tune to a softer side, trying to convince her to drop the charges.

Selena knew she now had the upper hand. She could possibly drag this out until the divorce was final, and be done with Paul without even having to be around him again. She was hurt that she didn't have anyone to confide in. Tamara, her very own sister had set her up and would be gaining from her divorce, and she had treated Andrea so badly when she assumed she was the one who had told Nadiyah about Zuri, that she was too embarrassed to call her.

She knew that Andrea deserved an apology, but she was going through so much, that she couldn't even muster up the words to make it sound sincere. She decided to call Nadiyah and let her know what had happened. She didn't care for her or her devious scheme, but knew she held the key to getting her out of this messy marriage.

Nadiyah answered on the first ring, and Selena rolled her eyes as she listened to her entire speech as she answered.

"N. Angela Owens, Attorney at Law. How may I assist you?"

"Nadiyah, it's Selena. I needed to let you know that Paul was arrested last night for assaulting me. Will this help speed the divorce up at all?"

Nadiyah explained that this would definitely work in her favor, and advised Selena that she would also file for sole custody of Zuri now that he had been charged with abuse. She noted that most judges showed great sympathy for battered wives, and usually granted them what they wanted in divorce cases like these. Selena was excited, even with all the sorrow and all the deceit that had been thrown her way. She was almost where she had set out to be since the day she found out Tamara had lied to her– happy and peaceful.

Over the next few weeks, contact with Paul was minimal. He would call every few days to hear Zuri's voice and beg Selena to rethink pressing charges. He mentioned how much money he could miss out on if word got out that he was an abuser. Selena couldn't care less. She was happy walking away with the $6,500,000.00 that she would receive if all went well, and that was with Nadiyah and Tamara's fee already deducted.

That would be more than enough to relocate and invest some money while she waited for the perfect opportunity to pursue Omar and live happily ever after. She knew it would work. Omar didn't call often, but he called at the right times, and that always brightened Selena's day. She knew that it was only because of the situation with her being married and him working out his contracts, and she didn't mind. She wanted him to get his money in order, so that when it was time to make it right, she and Zuri would be well taken care of.

Paul had never put Selena's name on the house, so she wasn't entitled to it, and that was fine. It was less time and worry to have to put the house on the market before she left for Florida. She had even decided to sign her home that was being rented by Andrea over to her. She thought it was the least she could do. Andrea had been a true friend to Selena, and she deserved it.

It was now June, and first up was the criminal hearing for Paul. Selena walked into the courtroom with her hair parted down the middle, bone straight. Her makeup was flawless. She wore a navy blue Tahari dress. It was fitted, but professional. Her toes were polished a pastel pink and looked perfect in the silver strappy BCBG sandals.

On the stand, she was emotional and recounted different occasions in which Paul was either physically or mentally abusive. She even suggested that he was sexually aggressive at times when she did not want to have sex.

She was cross examined by the defense, and their focal point was why she hadn't ever called the police or made anyone aware of the situation prior to when the divorce was filed.

Her answer was simple. "I was scared, and that last fight was the most violent that we had ever had. I always assumed that my husband was just stressed and an arm grab or occasional slap was all that would happen, but he almost choked me to death that day. And what made it worse, was that he…" Selena held her head down and began to wail before she finally finished, "…spit in my face."

"No further questions," yelled the stocky defense attorney as she sat down quickly and turned to Paul.

Paul's face was emotionless and he stared at Selena the entire time she sat on the stand. Selena knew that look. Paul was pissed, and him being pissed made Selena feel that much better. She stepped down off the stand and breezed past the table where Paul sat. She hoped he could smell her Flowerbomb, as he would never in life get to smell it again.

Paul was found guilty on the assault charges, and because he had no prior record, was sentenced to 2 years' probation and an anger management class. The restraining order remained in effect and would be that way for the next year. Nadiyah was able to get the initial divorce hearing scheduled two weeks after the criminal case.

Selena's demands were simple. She wanted half, which meant $7,500,000.00, sole custody of Zuri with supervised visits, and for the restraining order to remain active. The defense agreed to the terms, except for the sole custody. They wanted joint, which could be granted in several ways. It could mean every weekend, every other week, summers, there were many variations on joint custody. Selena knew if joint was granted, she would have to go by the rules and it would be hard to move to Florida if Paul would be entitled to see Zuri every weekend.

She knew that what was granted would determine whether or not she would have to reveal that Paul was not really Zuri's father. She knew if it was revealed, they would definitely shoot to give her less money, if any at all, just on the grounds of her lack of credibility. All she could do was wait it out and pray for the best.

CHAPTER 19

The day had come. Nadiyah and Selena had met briefly on the bench outside of the courtroom and were now heading in to hear the judge's ruling on their divorce and custody. Selena was surprised to see Andrea sitting outside the courtroom where the hearing would be held. Selena had sent Andrea an email a week ago, apologizing and acknowledging her for being a true friend. She had let Andrea know that the divorce was underway, and that the final hearing was today.

Andrea reached out to hug Selena, and Selena began to cry. Andrea smelled great. She had to be wearing Cashmere Mist by Donna Karan. Selena was happy to know that she was right, and that Andrea had stopped wearing that horrid J.LO perfume. Selena wiped her tears before she walked into the courtroom to hear her fate.

Paul sat with his lawyer in a light gray suit, a baby blue shirt, and gray and blue tie. He never made eye contact with Selena, but she knew he wanted to. The lawyers went back and forth for almost an hour with different numbers, dates, and state laws. Selena wanted it to be over.

Nadiyah made it clear that Selena had plans to relocate to another state, and would prefer longer bouts of shared custody versus days or week by week, if any at all. She was confused by all the legal jargon and was ready to hear the ruling. Her stomach was in knots, and as usual, when she was anxious, her armpits were soaking wet through the cream silk ruffled blouse that she wore.

The judge was finally ready to rule. Selena had tuned out everyone except the Caucasian male that appeared to be in his sixties with the black robe and glasses that sat on the tip of his nose. The ruling was in, and Selena cried tears of joy. It was all in her favor—the money, the custody, and the restraining order.

Although Selena would have custody, Paul would be entitled to 60 days each summer. This was perfect. He would have Zuri the remainder of the summer, which would give Selena enough time to get everything in order for their move. She knew in her heart that Paul would never harm Zuri, and was comfortable with the judgment.

She didn't think much of other summers that Zuri would need to spend with Paul, because Selena planned to be with Omar in Florida by then, and Paul would be out of the picture for good. She knew once Omar was able to spend some time with Zuri, he would fall in love and want his family. She would already have the money from Paul and wouldn't care if he found out that Zuri wasn't his.

Selena felt no sympathy for Paul as he sat in the court-room with tears rolling down his face. She walked gingerly out of the courtroom to a waiting Andrea with whom she hi-fived and hugged.

The next few weeks were hectic for Selena. She had to abide by the court order and send Zuri with Paul, move out of Paul's home, and pay her debt to Nadiyah. She had decided to stay with Andrea at the town home while she searched for a home in Miami. Andrea was a big help, when she wasn't at work.

Every day, Selena sat on the internet trying to find the perfect home for her and her princess. She looked at town homes, single homes, and even condominiums. She had narrowed her selections down to three, and would be going to see them as soon as her money hit her account.

* * * * *

Selena couldn't believe it. She called her bank to check her balance and she heard the magic words, "Your available balance is seven million, five hundred thousand dollars and zero cents."

She screamed and began to jump up and down on the couch. Andrea came running downstairs wondering what was wrong but quickly realized that today must have been what the two had been referring to as "PAYDAY". They celebrated by popping open a bottle of Pink Moscato and grooving to the radio. The first order of business was to pay Nadiyah. She wanted that headache off her back, and fast. She texted her and informed her that she had received the money and would meet with her the following day to receive all the account information necessary in order to transfer over her payment.

Everything went smoothly with Nadiyah. She received the account transfer and would be handling whatever she needed to handle with Tamara on her end. Selena was finally free of their drama.

She surprised Andrea with the deed to the house. Andrea had been there for Selena through this whole ordeal, even when she had treated her badly. The least she could do was make sure she had a permanent home to call her own. Andrea was grateful, and vowed to take care of the home.

Time had flown, and in just two days, Paul would be returning Zuri to Selena. She had missed her, everything from her scent, to the curls in her hair. She couldn't wait to kiss her fluffy cheeks and fall asleep holding the love of her life. Her original plans were to go see some homes in Florida while Zuri was away, but she had been in contact with Omar and they had agreed to see each other and for Selena to bring Zuri.

Andrea would be traveling with Selena and Zuri. Omar still didn't want to be seen with just Selena and the baby for anyone to begin speculating. If any questions were to arise, it was agreed that Andrea would be labeled his female companion, and Selena and Zuri as just their friends. Selena was a little annoyed that she and Zuri were still a secret, but she was confident that once he spent time with her, he would want nothing more than a family.

Zuri was beautiful, energetic, and loveable. What made it even better was that she was his. There was no denying it, and Selena couldn't wait for the day when he would accept and appreciate his family.

Paul and Selena met on neutral ground with a mediator present. The exchange from Paul to Selena was quick and quiet. They each spoke gently and barely made eye contact. Paul held Zuri tightly, kissing her face and stroking her hair before he handed her to Selena.

Zuri's face lit up with excitement to see her mother. She leaned her lips close to Selena and left a wet sticky kiss due to the cherry taffy she was sucking on. Selena felt no pain for Paul. She still had flashbacks of him spitting on her as she lay on the ground struggling to breathe.

Paul yelled out to Zuri that he loved her as they began walking in separate directions.

Zuri turned her head and began to wave as she said, "Bye Dada."

CHAPTER 20

The weather in Miami was fabulous, but Selena was tired of house hunting already, and it was only the first day. Andrea was a huge help, especially with Zuri. She was quite the busy body, and it was hard to try to conduct business, chasing after a one year old. They were all tired and hungry when Selena decided to end the home search for the day. They would meet back with the agent the following day. They weren't going to meet with Omar until later in the afternoon, so they ate and decided to go back to the hotel to rest until Omar arrived at home and was ready for them to come over.

It was almost six o'clock when Selena was awakened by the sound of her cell phone ringing. She glanced over and noticed that Andrea and Zuri were asleep as well. She quickly walked into the living room of their suite. It was Omar. He said he was close to the hotel they were staying in, and would pick them up to go over to his place.

Selena was ecstatic. She quickly woke Andrea up, and they freshened up, woke up the baby, and waited for Omar to call when he was downstairs.

After they were settled in the black Cadillac Escalade driven by Omar's Italian driver, Fredo, Omar couldn't take his eyes off Zuri. She looked more like him every day, in Selena's eyes. The summer sun had turned her bright complexion to beautiful bronze. Her smile was electrifying, and Selena enjoyed every moment of watching Zuri interact with her father.

They had finally arrived at Omar's home. He had moved since Selena had last been in Florida. He now owned a single family home. It was still modest, for him to be an NBA superstar, but that was Omar's personality in general. He wasn't flashy at all.

Omar was the first one out of the SUV. Selena stared at his beautiful shaped eyes and admired his chiseled body. She thought of how perfect their family would be. Omar reached out his hands for Zuri, and she didn't hesitate. She plopped right in his arms as if she belonged there.

Omar opened his front door and Selena was impressed with the decor. It was lavish and coordinated, very different from Omar's condo. Selena complimented the home and stated she would wait a while before he took her on the tour.

Omar laughed and invited them to tour the house right then. Zuri was still at peace on his hip. The house was beautiful. It was reminiscent of a Japanese steak house with its rich red hues, Kimonu influenced curtains, and huge fish tanks with beautiful tropical fish.

They headed up the stairs, and Selena smelled it. It was Burberry Touch. The smell brought a smile to Selena's face as they viewed the additional four bedrooms before they headed to the master suite. The smell of Burberry intensified, as they grew closer to the master suite. She couldn't believe that Omar now wore cologne. She knew she had influenced him in some way.

Omar turned the knob to his bedroom door, and

Selena and Andrea almost passed out. Omar stood with his mouth open, then turned and passed Zuri to Selena. He was clearly embarrassed, and Selena was at a loss for words.

"Well, hello, we meet again," Omar's guest stated sarcastically.

There lying in Omar's king sized bed was Everett Carter, Omar's agent. He stood up naked, exposing his beautiful body and quickly wrapped a towel around his waist.

"Surprise, surprise. Omar you didn't mention that ya baby momma would be visiting," he snapped.

"What's up with you? What are you doing in my bed?" Omar nervously asked.

His attempts to act as if this was something out of the ordinary were lame. Selena saw right through it. It all made sense now. This is why Omar lacked the compassion towards her that she longed for and why Everett was so angry when Omar came to take the paternity test. Selena couldn't believe it. Omar was gay, which meant that Zuri's father was a homosexual.

Her head started spinning. Her life was again in turmoil. She felt weak. Andrea still hadn't closed her mouth, but was able to grab Zuri, who had begun to cry, from Selena. She motioned for her friend to just walk away. She tugged her slightly, but Selena barely moved. She then slowly began to step back out of the bedroom, staring at Everett, who was smirking at her.

Omar stood still, staring at Zuri who was in Andrea's arms. Selena finally turned to walk away, and all she heard was Omar whisper quietly, "I'm sorry."

TO BE CONTINUED…

G STREET CHRONICLES
PRESENTS

LIFE
A SHORT STORY

BY
Aaliyah Shabazz

G STREET Essence

A childhood full of dysfunction and unsightly events is enough to make the sweetest person bitter. By the time Julisa is a teenager, the two most important people in her life are gone, and depending on her mother would get her nowhere.

Her new college environment brings out her desire to explore and losing her virginity to the campus jock scars her for life. Allowing her unfortunate situation to control her social life and finding herself in one failed relationship after another leads her to ending her streak with a suicide attempt.

She completely gives up on love and happiness until she meets Jason, her knight in shining armor. He accepts everything about her and loves her wholeheartedly. The problem—Jason has a woman in his life who will do any and everything to control and protect him, including keeping his own child from him.

Once married, Julisa and her mother-in-law fight for Jason's complete attention. Secrets from the past ignite a storm of emotions for all parties and in the end, everyone's LIFE is drastically changed.

Money, lies, control, and love create the perfect recipe for murder. Who will live to tell?

We'd like to thank you for supporting G Street Chronicles and invite you to join our social networks. Please be sure to post a review when you're finished reading.

Facebook
G Street Chronicles Fan Page
G Street Chronicles CEO Exclusive Readers Group

Twitter
@GStreetChronicl

My Space
G Street Chronicles

Email us and we'll add you to our mailing list
fans@gstreetchronicles.com

George Sherman Hudson, CEO
Shawna A., COO